THE FOLGER LIBRARY SHAKESPEARE

Designed to make Shakespeare's classic plays available to the general reader, each edition contains a reliable text with modernized spelling and punctuation, scene-by-scene plot summaries, and explanatory notes clarifying obscure and obsolete expressions. An interpretive essay and accounts of Shakespeare's life and theater form an instructive preface to each play.

Louis B. Wright, General Editor, was the Director of the Folger Shakespeare Library from 1948 until his retirement in 1968. He is the author of *Middle-Class Culture in Elizabethan England, Religion and Empire, Shakespeare for Everyman,* and many other books and essays on the history and literature of the Tudor and Stuart periods.

Virginia Lamar, Assistant Editor, served as research assistant to the Director and Executive Secretary of the Folger Shakespeare Library from 1946 until her death in 1968. She is the author of *English Dress in the Age of Shakespeare* and *Travel and Roads in England,* and coeditor of William Strachey's *Historie of Travell into Virginia Britania.*

The Folger Shakespeare Library

A Folger Library General Reader's Edition

THE TRAGEDY OF

DOCTOR FAUSTUS

By

CHRISTOPHER MARLOWE

WASHINGTON SQUARE PRESS
PUBLISHED BY POCKET BOOKS NEW YORK

A Washington Square Press Publication of
POCKET BOOKS, a division of Simon & Schuster, Inc.
1230 Avenue of the Americas, New York, N.Y. 10020

ISBN: 0-671-50977-2

First Pocket Books printing October, 1959

25   24   23   22   21   20

WASHINGTON SQUARE PRESS, WSP and colophon are
registered trademarks of Simon & Schuster, Inc.

Printed in the U.S.A.

Preface

This edition of *Doctor Faustus* is designed to make available a readable text of one of the most famous plays by the Elizabethan dramatist Christopher Marlowe, whose works were so influential in the development of the English drama. Explanatory notes have been included to clarify words and phrases which might be obscure to the modern reader. A brief biographical essay on Christopher Marlowe, which attempts to place him in his period, is also included. Readers desiring more detailed information should refer to the titles under "References for Further Reading."

All illustrations are from material in the collections of the Folger Library.

L. B. W.
V. A. L.

June 4, 1959

Christopher Marlowe and His Plays

Christopher Marlowe, whose life ended when he was twenty-nine, is one of the most significant of Elizabethan dramatists; he was a pioneer and innovator in addition to being a poet of genius. When he began to write for the stage, plays were still relatively crude and naïve productions, frequently written in old-fashioned jog-trot verse. Marlowe introduced a powerful and flexible blank verse and centered interest in the portrayal of some strong character in each of his tragedies. The young Shakespeare was to observe Marlowe's practice and profit by imitation. Marlowe's plays represent a great step forward in literary skill and dramatic power.

The son of a Canterbury shoemaker who was a substantial citizen of the community, Marlowe was born on February 6, 1564, a little over ten weeks before Shakespeare's birth. He attended the King's School, Canterbury, and in 1581 matriculated at Corpus Christi College, Cambridge, on a scholarship established by Archbishop Parker. He received his B.A. degree in 1584 and the M.A. in 1587. As the holder of one of the Parker scholarships, Marlowe was expected to take holy orders and to enter the clergy. At some point in his theological studies, however, he was diverted from orthodoxy and chose the stage instead of the pulpit for the expression of his ideas.

In June of the year that he received his M.A. degree, the Privy Council wrote a letter to the authorities at Cambridge stating that it had been reported that Christopher Marlowe planned to go "beyond seas to Rheims," then a center for disaffected English Catholics, but the Privy Council hoped that this rumor could be "allayed by all possible means" because "it was not her Majesty's pleasure that anyone employed as he had been in matters touching the benefit of his country should be defamed by those who are ignorant in the affairs he went about [engaged in]."

It is quite remarkable that the Queen's Privy Council should thus concern itself with a twenty-three-year-old divinity student at Cambridge unless he had performed some unusual service. What this service was we do not know, but the tone of the letter suggests that for a brief period he may have been sent overseas on some confidential mission. Like other events in Marlowe's life, this episode remains unexplained. In the light of later events, it has been suggested that he was a spy in the service of Sir Francis Walsingham, principal secretary and head of Queen Elizabeth's secret service, but direct evidence is lacking.

Shortly after leaving the university, Marlowe took up residence in London. What he did for a livelihood is unknown to us, but that he turned his hand to dramatic writing is a certainty. The plays that have survived from his pen were not sufficient to support him, and he must have had some other source of income. He was part of a brilliant circle of young men who included Sir Walter Raleigh; Thomas Hariot, the mathematician and scientist; Thomas Nashe, the pamphleteer; and other writers. For a time he had as a roommate Thomas Kyd, playwright and author of *The Spanish Tragedy*, a sensational drama. Kyd was later to testify that among other iniquities, Marlowe had a violent temper and was "intemperate and of a cruel heart."

A murder in which Marlowe was involved on September 18, 1589, indicates that Kyd may have had some grounds for this characterization of his roommate. On that day Marlowe met by chance in Hog Lane, not far from Shoreditch where he himself was living, a certain William Bradley, son of a Holborn innkeeper. A few weeks earlier Bradley had sworn out a warrant against Thomas Watson, poet and friend of Marlowe's, and two others, charging that he was in danger of his life from them. What Marlowe's quarrel was the evidence does not state, but as they were fighting with swords, Watson appeared and Bradley lunged at him. Watson ran him through and Bradley died before help could reach him. Both Marlowe and Watson were lodged in Newgate Prison, but Marlowe, who was not charged with actual murder himself, was released on October 1 on bail of forty pounds. Marlowe escaped punishment and Watson received a royal pardon in February, 1590. But Marlowe was not through with the law. On May 9, 1592, two constables from Shoreditch swore out a warrant against Marlowe requiring him to keep the peace. They alleged that they were in terror of their lives from him. That Marlowe was less than a placid poet is evident.

In the spring of 1593, Marlowe appears to have taken up residence in the household of Sir Thomas Walsingham at Scadbury near Chislehurst in Kent. Plague was raging in London and Walsingham's country house made a pleasant retreat. But once more Marlowe found himself in difficulties, this time with the Privy Council, which undertook to investigate a serious charge of atheism and blasphemy that had been made by Thomas Kyd, perhaps to excuse himself. On May 12, 1593, Kyd had been arrested on a charge of posting "lewd and mutinous libels" on a churchyard wall. When his room was searched, papers were found containing "atheistic" writings. Atheism in this period was a loose term that could cover almost any departure from orthodoxy. Kyd claimed that the papers had belonged to Marlowe and had become mixed with his own when the two shared a room and both dramatists were writing for the acting company of a certain unidentified lord, probably Lord Strange. Kyd also charged that Marlowe "would persuade men of quality to go unto the King of Scots . . . where . . . he told me . . . he meant to be." King James VI of Scotland was already being talked of as the possible successor to Queen Elizabeth and some Englishmen were anxiously looking toward Scotland and, as an insurance for the future, were hoping for favor with the Scottish King. A few days after Kyd's statement, a professional informer, one Richard Baines, came forward with a whole battery of "the most horrible blasphemes and damnable opinions" attributed to Marlowe, including a statement that the Sacraments "would have been much better being administered in a tobacco pipe." The charges were sufficiently grave for the Privy Council on May 18 to issue a warrant to its messenger, Henry Maunder, "to repair to the house of Mr. Thomas Walsingham in Kent, or to any other place where he shall understand Christopher Marlowe to be remaining, and by virtue thereof to apprehend and bring him to the Court in his company." Twelve days after this warrant was issued, Fate intervened to prevent a hearing of the charges against Marlowe. On May 30, he was murdered in the tavern of Eleanor Bull in Deptford.

The circumstances surrounding the death of Christopher Marlowe are related in the testimony at the coroner's inquest. Marlowe, who had accepted an invitation from one Ingram Friser to a "feast," had arrived at Eleanor Bull's house at about ten in the morning. Two others joined them, Nicholas Skeres and Robert Poley. All three of these men enjoyed unsavory reputations. Friser and Skeres had been mixed up in confidence games and various swindles, apparently with the connivance of one who ought to have been above such trickery, no other than Sir Thomas Walsingham. Poley was a secret agent recently returned from some mission abroad. He too had been involved in shady transactions.

Clearly, Marlowe was in bad company, but we have only conjecture to explain his friendship with sharpers and spies. They dined in the middle of the day and, after a walk in the garden, about six o'clock they returned to the private room that they were occupying and had supper together. After supper, Marlowe lay down on a bed while the other three sat on a bench at the table in front of him and played backgammon. Friser sat between Skeres and Poley with his back to Marlowe. Hanging from his belt was a dagger. Marlowe, who had begun to quarrel with Friser over the tavern bill, seized the dagger from his belt and struck him in the head with it. Friser, with his legs under the table, wedged between Poley and Skeres, was about to be slain by Marlowe, he swore before the coroner, but he managed to twist around, grab Marlowe's hand, and thrust the dagger back upon him in such a manner that it entered his forehead and gave him "then and there a mortal wound over his right eye of the depth of two inches and the width of one inch, of which mortal wound the aforesaid Christopher Morley [Marlowe] then and there instantly died."

This is the stark account at the inquest proceedings which Professor Leslie Hotson discovered in 1925. Marlowe was buried on June 1 in the

churchyard of St. Nicholas, Deptford, and the
parish register incorrectly noted that he was
slain by "ffrancis ffrezer." On June 28, Ingram
Friser received a full pardon for the murder. He
lived to a ripe old age and died a churchwarden.

Since the discovery of the inquest papers,
scholars have speculated upon Marlowe's end
and have wondered whether the testimony is
all that it purports to be. Why was Marlowe keep-
ing company with these three men, two of whom
were associates in shady enterprises backed by
Walsingham, and one of whom was a government
secret agent of doubtful reputation? Friser was
high in the confidence of Lady Walsingham, who
is supposed to have been engaged in clandestine
correspondence with the King of Scotland. Was
Marlowe, as Kyd charged, also in correspondence
with Scottish agents? Did he know too much and
was he murdered to get an inconvenient and ir-
responsible talker out of the way? These are
questions that cannot be answered in the light
of present evidence, but Marlowe's career and
death suggest some mystery that is likely to
continue to haunt students of Elizabethan literary
history. The fantastic notion that he was not
really killed but was smuggled away and lived
to write the plays attributed to Shakespeare is

based on nothing except vain imaginings and has nothing to commend it.

Fascinating as are surmises about Marlowe the victim of a mysterious murder, we are more concerned with Marlowe the poet and dramatist, who at the age of twenty-nine had set a new fashion in stage plays. He had begun to write before he left Cambridge, and by the end of 1587 the two parts of *Tamburlaine* had won the plaudits of London audiences. In quick succession came *Doctor Faustus* (1588), *The Jew of Malta* (1589), *Edward the Second* (*ca.* 1592), *The Massacre at Paris* (1593), and *Dido, Queen of Carthage*, written in collaboration with Thomas Nashe (*ca.* 1593). He may have had a hand in one or two other plays. The dates of composition and first acting cannot be given with certainty, but this appears to be the most plausible chronology. In addition to his dramas he made translations from Lucan's *Pharsalia* and Ovid's *Amores*, and from Musaeus he retold a famous classical story in his own *Hero and Leander*, an unfinished poem that George Chapman completed.

Marlowe's poetry is the work of a young man of the Renaissance rebellious against many traditions and yet strongly influenced by the literary heritage from the ancient world. At Cambridge he had broken with Christian orthodoxy and henceforth exemplified the angry young man of his day, flouting the unco guid and stirring the animosities of conventional religious folk. After his death, Puritan preachers like Thomas Beard would point a moral and adorn their tales of the untimely ends of evildoers with garbled accounts of Marlowe's end. During his years at Cambridge he read widely in classical literature and ranged beyond into geography, history, and philosophy—wherever his inquiring mind took him. Upon this storehouse of material he drew when he sat down to write his plays and poetry. To his work he gave a pagan twist, for Marlowe is an example of the influence of the pagan Renaissance. He would have found himself at home among some of the Italian writers of a previous generation.

One of the characteristics of the Renaissance was its intellectual curiosity and its belief in the potentialities of the human mind. It was a youthful age to which nothing seemed impossible. The age also placed a new emphasis on the individual and men learned to cultivate their capacities and to develop all sides of their personalities. The resources of the mind seemed as limitless as the great world, which the discoveries beyond the seas had more than doubled. The explorations of Tudor mariners did more than expand the geographical limits of the planet, and the new discoveries in science and developments in technology went beyond mere material advances. All of these things stirred men's imaginations and led them to believe that the infinite was attainable.

Marlowe's tragedies are studies in the search for the infinite, even if it is nothing better than infinite revenge and infinite evil as in *The Jew of Malta*. The two parts of *Tamburlaine* portray the career of a despot struggling for infinite power. The interest throughout focuses upon the Scythian shepherd-king as he contemplates the world which he means to conquer and repeats to himself:

> Is it not passing brave to be a king
> And ride in triumph through Persepolis?

And a little later Tamburlaine tells Cosroe, brother of the defeated King of Persia:

> The thirst of reign and sweetness of a crown
>
> .   .   .   .
>
> Moved me to manage arms against thy state.
> What better precedent than mighty Jove?
> Nature that framed us of four elements,
> Warring within our breasts for regiment,

Doth teach us all to have aspiring minds;
Our souls, whose faculties can comprehend
The wondrous architecture of the world
And measure every wand'ring planet's course,
Still climbing after knowledge infinite
And always moving as the restless spheres,
Wills us to wear ourselves, and never rest,
Until we reach the ripest fruit of all,
That perfect bliss and sole felicity,
The sweet fruition of an earthly crown.

Marlowe puts these words into Tamburlaine's
mouth but he is speaking in his own proper
person as a young man of the Renaissance. The
"sweet fruition of an earthly crown" is merely
the symbol of all the infinite ambition that he
himself felt for the attainment of the impossible.

In *Doctor Faustus*, the greatest of his poetic
conceptions, he provides a study of the scholar
in search of unlimited knowledge and the power
that knowledge may confer. Even more than in
Tamburlaine, we feel that Marlowe is thinking
of himself in the role of Faustus, the rebel against
conventional university learning, the rebel who
was willing to sell his soul to the devil for knowledge that was forbidden to less daring philosophers.

The theme of the man who makes a compact

with the devil is old in folklore. The particular version that took shape in the Faust legend appeared in print in Germany in 1587 as *Das Faustbuch* and was translated into English as *The Historie of the Damnable Life and Deserved Death of Dr. John Faustus.* The earliest extant edition of the English translation dates from 1592 but there is evidence of an edition before this which Marlowe is believed to have used, for episodes in the English Faust book, which do not appear in the German original, correspond with passages in the play. The name of Dr. Faustus may have come from an actual person, a certain Dr. Johannes Faustus who took a degree of doctor of divinity at Heidelberg University in 1509. Several men, however, bearing the name Faust, and in some fashion associated in the popular mind with magic, alchemy, astrology, and related activities, appear in German allusions in the first half of the sixteenth century. A composite of much of this legendary material was gathered up in *Das Faustbuch* and was transmitted thence to English and other literatures. In modern literature the legend reached its greatest exemplification in Goethe's *Faust.*

Marlowe gave the legend an interpretation characteristic of his own taste and personality. When the play opens, we see Faustus in his study surveying the state of knowledge and trying to decide which of the learned disciplines he will follow. Logic, medicine, law, divinity: all of these are inadequate for his towering ambition. He wants all knowledge, the ability to plumb the mysteries yet withheld from man, and the superhuman power that such knowledge will bring. The only way to attain this ambition is by magic, and the acquisition of the power of magic can be achieved only through a bargain made with the devil. Faustus is willing to pay the price, and makes the required compact.

All of this conveyed much more horror to an Elizabethan audience than it does to us, for Elizabethans by and large believed implicitly in such bargains. Indeed, the black magic of witchcraft was all around them, and it was no uncommon occurrence to attribute to witchcraft phenomena that could not be explained by other means. About *Doctor Faustus* a legend developed that during a performance at Exeter, in one scene in which Faustus called up devils, the actors counted one more devil than the scene called for and realized that Satan himself was in their midst. In terror, they stopped the play; the audience bolted from the playing place; and the actors quitted the town next morning. According to another story, Edward Alleyn, the actor who played the title role in *Doctor Faustus,* was himself so scared by a similar appearance of a veritable devil in a play by Shakespeare, that he made a vow that resulted in his founding Dulwich College. Witches and devils were real to an Elizabethan audience, and when Faustus abjured God and signed his soul away, their blood ran cold.

Critics have objected that Faustus, having gained infinite knowledge, made paltry use of his power in the play, and that the tricks performed were far beneath Marlowe's lofty conception of the part. One explanation is that Marlowe was hampered by the limitations of his own stage and the necessity of presenting something visual to his audiences. Another explanation is that we do not know precisely how much of the surviving play is Marlowe's and how much of the clownery and horseplay may have been added by later adapters. For *Doctor Faustus* has come down to us in a very corrupt state.

Although Marlowe's *Doctor Faustus* survives in only a garbled state, it contains poetic passages that reflect the feeling and intensity that Marlowe demonstrates elsewhere in his writings. Into Faustus' mouth he puts words that might apply to the poet himself:

Have I not made blind Homer sing to me
Of Alexander's love and Oenon's death,
And hath not he that built the walls of Thebes
With ravishing sound of his melodious harp
Made music with my Mephistophilis?
Why should I die, then, or basely despair?
I am resolved Faustus shall ne'er repent.
Come, Mephistophilis, let us dispute again
And argue of divine astrology.
Tell me, are there many heavens above the moon?
Are all celestial bodies but one globe,
As is the substance of this centric earth?

Marlowe in *Doctor Faustus* goes beyond the
sensuous and colorful verse of *Hero and Leander,*
where he seems to be playing with words as a
Renaissance painter might use his colors for the
attainment of gorgeous effects. In *Doctor Faustus*
he reaches new lyrical heights in passages where
he is concerned with the infinite reaches of the
human mind. When he invokes "divine astrology"
as in the foregoing passage, he means something
more than the word connotes today. He is probing
into the mysteries of the universe where he can
find revelations worth the price of his immortal
soul.

In another passage of lyric intensity when he
calls up Helen of Troy, he transcends sensual

delight and Her... ...ecomes the symbol of intellectual pleasure a... ...e was also the acme of physical delight:

Was this the face that launche... a thousand ships
And burnt the topless towers of Ilium?
Sweet Helen, make me immortal with a kiss.
Her lips sucks forth my soul—see where it flies!
Come, Helen, come, give me my soul again.
Here will I dwell, for heaven is in these lips
And all is dross that is not Helena.

.   .   .   .

O thou art fairer than the evening air
Clad in the beauty of a thousand stars!
Brighter art thou than flaming Jupiter
When he appeared to hapless Semele,
More lovely than the monarch of the sky
In wanton Arethusa's azured arms,
And none but thou shalt be my paramour!

A tenet of Renaissance Platonic philosophy taught that from earthly love one might rise to a perception of heavenly beauty, as Edmund Spenser showed in his *Four Hymns*. In Helen's beauty Marlowe found something beyond the satisfaction of physical love. To the youthful and iconoclastic poet, that too was worth the price of Faustus'— or his own—soul.

Although Marlowe lived write only a handful of plays, the English stage would be the greater for them. His melodious verse, the "mighty line" that Ben Jonson described, would forever influence English poetic drama. One greater than he, William Shakespeare, would learn from him and bring the blank verse line to perfection as a medium for dramatic expression.

PUBLICATION AND STAGE HISTORY OF
Doctor Faustus

The Stationer Thomas Bushell registered for publication "A book called the play of *Doctor Faustus*" in the Stationers' Register in 1601. A quarto may have been printed in that year, but if so, no copy is known to survive. The earliest printed version is the quarto of 1604, which was reprinted in 1609 and 1611. In 1616, an entirely new and greatly expanded version appeared. The 1616 quarto shows additions by play-doctors hired by Philip Henslowe, owner of the Rose Theatre, where the Lord Admiral's Men played. Edward Alleyn, Henslowe's son-in-law and part-owner with him, was one of the chief actors in the Lord Admiral's company. It was Alleyn who first played the roles of Tamburlaine, Faustus, and Barabas in *The Jew of Malta.* Henslowe's *Diary* records a payment of £4 on November 22, 1602, to William Bird and Samuel Rowley, two hack writers, for additions to *Doctor Faustus.* The 1604 quarto contains interpolations that Marlowe could not have inserted (including an allusion to Dr. Lopez who was accused of plotting to poison the Queen in 1594), and these additions may be the work of Bird and Rowley. But the play was evidently worked over more than once and by the time of the 1616 version it showed many changes.

Reprintings of the 1616 version occurred in 1619, 1620, 1624, 1628, 1631, and 1663. None of the later quartos have any authority and they merely perpetuate corruptions. The texts of *Faustus* are so bad that it is impossible to tell precisely what Marlowe wrote. Critics are inclined to believe that much of the clownery was inserted by later adapters.

The present edition follows the practice of many other editors in basing the text on the 1604 quarto with some corrections from the 1616 quarto. The clownery of the 1604 edition has been retained, even though some of it may owe little to the original author. The 1604 quarto does not divide the play into the customary five acts with their scenes, but the present edition follows conventional practice in breaking the play into scenes.

No records of performance before 1594 have survived, but between 1594 and 1598 Henslowe notes frequent (and profitable) productions of the play. Contemporary allusions also indicate that Faustus and the devils had become popular characters on the stage. The play had frequent revivals during the next half-century, and after the Restoration it was one of the plays that held the stage. Thomas Betterton, the famous actor of Shakespearean roles during this period, played Faustus. During the eighteenth century the play degenerated into a farce or a sensational stage spectacle, and Faustus even became the chief character of a puppet show. Toward the end of the nineteenth century, dramatic taste had improved, and producers returned to closer adaptations of the original. Sir Henry Irving chose to play Mephistophilis in a spectacular adaptation of the play at the Lyceum Theatre in London in 1885. Other professional theatres acted adaptations from Marlowe, and the play has frequently appeared on academic and "little theatre" stages in modern times.

From early in the seventeenth century, Marlowe's *Doctor Faustus* was seen on German stages, and during the present century it has appeared from time to time in Germany. Goethe apparently had some indirect knowledge of Marlowe's play when he was composing his own play on the Faust theme.

THEATRE AND DRAMA IN MARLOWE'S TIME*

When Marlowe was a child, older types of drama that had been popular since the late Middle Ages could still be seen occasionally on provincial stages. Dramas based on Biblical stories beginning with the Creation and ending with the Day of Judgment, the so-called "mystery" plays, had very nearly died out, but the somewhat later morality plays which used personified abstractions as characters were still being acted at intervals. During the reign of Henry VIII, a type of play called an interlude gained in popularity and continued to be acted until the development of the full-length Elizabethan play. The term "interlude" is not precise and scholars debate about its meaning. Interludes were usually short dramatic pieces, frequently corresponding in length to a one-act play, and were often performed in the halls of

*Adapted by permission from a booklet published by the Folger Shakespeare Library, *Shakespeare's Theatre and the Dramatic Tradition* (Washington, 1958), by Louis B. Wright.

great houses, sometimes as part of the entertainment offered at a dinner for some visiting dignitary. They were secular in tone, though some interludes continued to use personified abstractions of a sort. In one of the most curious of the type, *A New Interlude and a Merry of the Nature of the Four Elements*, attributed to John Rastell and written soon after the accession of Henry VIII, we are treated to a long dramatized lesson in science.

The more popular interludes, however, abandoned teaching in favor of sheer entertainment; the best of the writers in this kind was John Heywood, who provided short comic plays and farces for Henry VIII and his noblemen. Although Heywood was not an innovator and was content to borrow from Chaucer and to adapt French farcical stories to dramatic form, his interludes have a freshness and a vitality not found in morality plays, with which they competed for favor. Among the better known of Heywood's interludes is the *Play of the Weather*, in which Jupiter decides to let people choose their own weather but has to return to arbitrary methods when no two can agree on what they want. Another of his interludes, the *Four P's*, exemplifies an ancient but still popular comic device, the contest to see who can tell the biggest lie.

Many interludes and belated morality plays on a wide variety of themes survive from the first half of the sixteenth century. They include political satires like John Skelton's *Magnificence* and Sir David Lindsay's *Satire of the Three Estates;* dramatized tracts concerned with religious controversy like John Bale's *God's Promises* and other works from his vitriolic pen; and plays entirely for entertainment, like those of Heywood and such embryonic comedies as *Tom Tyler and His Wife.* The secular interludes made a significant contribution to the comic tradition and the satiric moralities gave a new dramatic purpose to the stage. The somewhat amorphous drama of the early sixteenth century stimulated the continued development of a popular taste for plays.

The players of interludes did not confine their performances to the great halls of the nobility but often took to the road. Entries in the town records of the visits of players increased markedly in the 1530's and continued through the rest of the century. Scarcely a town was too small to have a visit from a group of strolling players, who frequently described themselves as the servants of some noble lord. This designation merely meant that the nobleman had consented to become the patron of the company of players and thus to lend them his name as a measure of protection against harassment from local authorities, for players occupied a low position in the social scale and were frequently classified in civic regulations with vagabonds and sturdy beggars, a situation that prevailed until Shakespeare's lifetime.

Although relics of the old types of drama cropped up now and then throughout the sixteenth century, by the early years of Elizabeth's reign mature secular drama had come into being. The earliest type to develop was comedy, partly because of a strong native tradition of comic stage situations and partly because the new learning of the Renaissance had familiarized academic audiences with Roman comedy. It was not mere chance that one of Shakespeare's earliest plays, *The Comedy of Errors,* was an adaptation from the *Menaechmi* of Plautus, for he may have remembered the Roman dramatist from his grammar school studies. As early as 1553, Nicholas Udall, a former headmaster at Eton, composed a play on a Roman model and gave it the title of *Ralph Roister Doister*. Though it owes much to Plautine comedy, it is recognizably English in spirit. Sometime about 1553–54, the students of Christ's College, Cambridge, saw performed in their college hall another English comedy, *Gammer Gurton's Needle*, by an unidentified "Mr. S., Master of Arts." This play is still amusing enough to gain an audience.

On January 18, 1562, two years before Marlowe was born, the young gentlemen of the Inner Temple, one of the Inns of Court where law students received their training, presented before Queen Elizabeth the first fully developed English tragedy of which we have record, *The Tragedy of Gorboduc.* The authors, Thomas Sackville, later Earl of Dorset, and Thomas Norton, modeled their play after the style of the Roman writer Seneca but they also showed a familiarity with Italian dramatists. Though Elizabethan drama had not yet reached full maturity, the forms of both tragedy and comedy were now established and the development of both types would show rapid progress during the next three decades to culminate in the work of Shakespeare and his contemporaries.

The growing demand for plays and the development of full-length drama had created such a need for professional playhouses by the late 1570's that in 1576 a cabinetmaker-turned-actor named James Burbage erected the first building in London designed exclusively for the use of players. To it he gave the descriptive name The Theatre. Its site was east of Finsbury Fields, a park area to the northward of the city proper, on land leased from one Giles Alleyn. Burbage had been careful to choose a site just outside the jurisdiction of the city authorities yet close enough to be accessible for playgoers. Within a year another playhouse called The Curtain (from the name of the estate on which it was located) opened nearby. London now had two professional public playhouses, both outside the city's jurisdiction. It was important to be beyond the reach of the aldermen of London, for they maintained an inveterate hostility to the players on the grounds that they caused disturbances, brought together crowds that spread the plague, lured apprentices from their work, and were generally ungodly.

An early attempt to open a playhouse within the city was made by Richard Farrant, Master of the Children of Windsor Chapel. For a long time the choirboys of Windsor Chapel, like the choirboys of the Chapel Royal and St. Paul's Cathedral, had been accustomed to performing plays and to taking part in other entertainments at Court. Farrant conceived the notion of renting a hall in part of the old Blackfriars Monastery and of fitting it up for a playhouse on the pretext of rehearsing plays to be performed before the Queen. Although the Blackfriars property was within the walls of the city of London, not far from St. Paul's Cathedral, it retained its ancient exemption from the jurisdiction of the city's aldermen. Even so, Farrant did not dare try to open a public theatre but announced that it would be a "private" house though open to paying customers. This distinction between "public" and "private" theatres would persist throughout the Elizabethan period. Farrant's subterfuge worked and he opened his playhouse late in 1576 or early in 1577. Despite trouble with his landlord his theatre was a modest success until his death in 1580. The Blackfriars Theatre operated for another four years under the direction of William Hunnis, Master of the Children of the Chapel Royal, with the help for a time of John Lyly, a young novelist and dramatist. There Lyly's own plays were performed by the boy actors.

From the time of the opening of the earliest formal theatres, the public and the private houses differed widely in physical characteristics and methods of staging. The public theatres, for all we know, may have been influenced in their shape and construction by the circular arenas, like those on the Bankside across the Thames, which were used for bull- and bear-baiting. A more significant influence on their architecture, however, came from the inns. Long before the erection of regular theatres, players had used the yards of inns, and in London certain inns like the Cross Keys, the Bell, and the Bull were noted as playing places for professional actors. At the inns, the players had been accustomed to set up a stage at one end of the open courtyard and to accommodate spectators in the courtyard, which was open to the weather, and in the surrounding galleries.

The public theatres for many years retained this open-courtyard feature. There the "groundlings" for the price of a penny could stand while more opulent spectators could pay a higher fee for the privilege of sitting in the galleries. Plays were performed in the daytime, beginning in the early afternoon, for the stage had no means of artificial lighting. The public theatres could not be used in the worst weather or in the dead of winter. The private houses were enclosed halls in which plays could be given at night. They could be used in winter and in all weathers. The stage was lighted by candles, lamps, or torches. The private houses were not private in the sense of restricting audiences to any special groups but prices were higher than in the public playhouses, a fact that may have given the private houses a somewhat more select audience.

A place of recreation long popular with the citizens of London was the Bankside, an extensive area on the Southwark side of the Thames and west of what is now Southwark Cathedral. Much of this territory consisted of land that had formerly belonged to the Church or the Crown, and the aldermen of London had no authority over certain areas like the Manor of Paris Garden and the Liberty of the Clink. These and other localities beyond the jurisdiction of the city became the sites for a variety of amusements.

To the Bankside, Londoners went to witness bear- and bull-baitings at arenas erected for the purpose. After one of the old arenas collapsed in 1583 with some loss of life, a polygonal amphitheatre called the New Bear Garden was erected. Other even less savory enticements brought Londoners to the Bankside. This area by the 1580's was attracting the interest of theatrical entrepreneurs. One of these was Philip Henslowe, the semiliterate but shrewd businessman who in 1587 was instrumental in building the Rose playhouse, not far from the Bear Garden. Henslowe has earned the gratitude of literary historians because he kept an account book, usually described as his *Diary*, which preserves much theatrical and dramatic history. His son-in-law, Edward Alleyn, was one of the most famous actors and stage managers of the day.

The popularity of Henslowe's Rose stimulated another businessman, Francis Langley, a goldsmith, to purchase the Manor of Paris Garden west of the site of the Rose and the Bear Garden. There he erected in 1595 a new theatre which he called the Swan. This playhouse is of interest to historians because in 1596 a Dutch priest, Johannes de Witt, saw a performance at the Swan and described the stage to a friend, Arend van Buchell, who made a drawing that is the earliest visual representation of an Elizabethan stage in use.

Because of its association with William Shakespeare, the best known of the Bankside theatres is the Globe. The Globe was erected in 1599, in part from timbers of The Theatre, which the lessees, Cuthbert and Richard Burbage, moved across the Thames on December 28, 1598, to a site in Maiden Lane which they had chosen when their landlord made trouble over the lease of The Theatre. To be owners of the new playhouse, the Burbages organized a stock company consisting of themselves and four actors including Shakespeare and John Heminges, who was later to be one of the editors of the 1623 collection of Shakespeare's plays. The theatre owners, or "house-keepers" as they were then called, received half the receipts from the galleries. The acting company received the other half and all the receipts taken at the door. Thus Shakespeare, who was a house-keeper, a member of the acting company, and a dramatist, received income from all three sources. The Globe was completed in 1599 and lasted until 1613, when it burned down after a piece of wadding from a cannon fired during a performance of *Henry VIII* ignited its thatched roof. A second Globe was soon erected to take its place. The first Globe is usually pictured as octagonal on the outside, but despite the octagonal pictures in seventeenth-century views of London, some evidence points to a circular shape. The interior may have been circular. The Globe was the model for the Fortune Theatre, which Henslowe and Alleyn erected in 1600 north of the city on the opposite side of Finsbury Fields from the site of The Theatre and The Curtain. In only one essential did they change the design. The Fortune was square. The builder's specifications for the Fortune, which have survived, provide the best existing information about Elizabethan theatrical construction.

A playhouse that combined the functions of a theatre with those of an arena for bear- and bull-baiting was the Hope, erected in 1613 on the site of the Bear Garden, which had fallen into decay and was torn down to make way for the new building. The owners of the Hope were Philip Henslowe and a partner, Jacob Meade. The contract which the partners signed with the carpenter-contractor exists and throws some light on its construction. The Hope had a portable stage which could be removed when the building was required for other purposes. Over the stage area was a permanent canopy. But details of the construction of the stage and the entry doors that we would like to have are omitted. The contract specifies that the contractor is to build the Hope "of such large compass, form, wideness, and height as the playhouse called the Swan."

One other public theatre needs to be mentioned. This was the Red Bull, built about 1605 in the upper end of St. John's Street, Clerkenwell, about a mile from the old Curtain. This theatre was a favorite with London apprentices and was the place where some of the more boisterous of Elizabethan plays were performed.

Almost as important as the Globe in the history of Shakespeare's company was the second Blackfriars Theatre. In 1596 James Burbage purchased a portion of the Frater building in the rambling old Blackfriars Monastery and remodeled it for a theatre. Like the earlier Blackfriars it was a covered hall, but it was more elaborately designed, with galleries for spectators and a better equipped stage at one end. The precise construction of the stage we do not know. Burbage leased the theatre for several years to the managers of the boy actors of the Chapel Royal, but in 1608, when the lease expired, a syndicate of seven actors, including Shakespeare, took it over. Henceforth Shakespeare's company operated the Blackfriars as a "private" theatre, but in actuality it was the playhouse regularly used by the company in winter.

Both the Blackfriars and the Globe stages, like other Elizabethan stages, were platform stages without the familiar proscenium arch of the modern theatre, and of course without a curtain to come down between the acts and at the end of the play. These stages also lacked painted and movable scenery, though Elizabethan theatres made considerably more use of stage properties than we have been led to believe. The question that has aroused the greatest controversy concerns the use of an inner stage and the location of entry doors and balconies in the back of the stage.

The Swan drawing shows a projecting platform stage with two doors flat against the rear wall. People, presumably spectators, are shown in the balcony over the rear stage doors. The Swan drawing also shows a canopy supported by columns over a portion of the stage and a room above that. The canopy and room above were characteristics of all the public theatres. The upper room, called the "tiring house," was used for dressing and storage. From a trap door in the canopy, called the "heavens," gods and angels might descend when the action required it.

Most modern reconstructions of the stage of the Globe provide an inner stage, useful for bedroom or "study" scenes, with an upper stage above it. Both of these are closed with curtains. Stage doors open obliquely on each side with boxes or balconies above. This type of construction would best suit a scene like the balcony scene in *Romeo and Juliet*. Some scholars insist that the inner stage was too deeply recessed to permit many in the audience to see properly, and that bedroom scenes must have been staged farther forward on the platform, with properties brought into use as they were required. There is no convincing evidence that the regular Elizabethan theatres were designed for performances in the round. There is much evidence for the use of an inner and upper stage with entry doors set either flat against the back or diagonally on the sides. It should be pointed out, however, that the text and directions of many plays seem to indicate the use of the main stage for scenes that editors like to relegate to an inner stage. Such use of the main stage suggests that necessary properties and equipment could be set up in advance and ignored by the audience until time for their use, as in the simultaneous-stage settings in medieval drama.

Where there are so many suggestions of both types of staging, one cannot escape the conclusion that usage varied, and that stage construction in the theatres may have differed in some important details. Actors have always been skilled in improvising, and Elizabethan players had to be unusually adroit in this respect in order to adapt their plays to a wide variety of conditions: performances in the great hall at Court, in a public theatre in the daytime, in a private theatre at night, or on some makeshift stage in a country town when the plague closed the London theatres and sent the actors strolling through the provinces.

During Shakespeare's lifetime, the principal theatres were occupied by companies of actors organized under the patronage of various titled personages. The company with which Shakespeare was associated for most of his active career had for its earliest patron Henry Carey, Lord Hunsdon, the Lord Chamberlain. Hence they were known as the Lord Chamberlain's Men. After the accession of James I, the King became their patron and they were known as the King's Men. They were the great rivals of the Lord Admiral's Men, managed by Henslowe and Alleyn. Competitors with all the adult companies were the child actors drawn from the choirboys of the Chapel Royal, Windsor, and St. Paul's. These actors are referred to in *Hamlet* as "an eyrie of children, little eyases, that cry out on the top of question and are most tyrannically clapped for't." The adult companies recruited some of their best impersonators of female roles from the children's companies, for the Elizabethan stage never employed women as players. That innovation had to wait until the Restoration.

Elizabethan acting must have been skillful and effective. To hold the attention of a restless and unruly audience in close proximity, the actors had to speak their lines well and simulate their parts to perfection. The impersonation of women's roles by boys seems to us the least satisfactory element in Elizabethan acting, but there is ample evidence that youths succeeded in these parts. No Elizabethan complained that a boy spoiled the role of Juliet.

Elizabethan audiences were not accustomed to the conventions of modern staging and did not expect realistic sets and colorful scenery in the professional playhouses. At Court, it is true, the masques were mounted with magnificent splendor —and at great cost—but these were spectacles for royalty, and few who witnessed plays in the theatres ever saw a masque. We have perhaps overemphasized the bareness of the Elizabethan stage and we may forget that Elizabethan producers made adequate use of stage properties. Nevertheless we are correct in insisting that Elizabethan plays were written primarily for the ear rather than the eye. It was not always necessary to stick up a board reading "The Forest of Arden" or some other locale. The poetry frequently conveyed the description adequately for the audience to comprehend both the place and the atmosphere that the dramatist wanted to suggest. In the age of Shakespeare poetic drama reached its greatest height, and one can speculate as to whether Shakespeare would have written so vividly if he could have left to the carpenter and the scene painter the effects that he achieved in words.

REFERENCES FOR FURTHER READING

Many readers will want suggestions for further reading about the Tudor and Stuart theatres as well as material on the history of the period. Detailed discussion of the development of the English stage in the periods covered may be found in the following monumental works: E. K. Chambers, *The Medieval Stage* (2 vols., Oxford, 1903); E. K. Chambers, *The Elizabethan Stage* (4 vols., Oxford, 1923); and Gerald E. Bentley, *The Jacobean and Caroline Stage* (5 vols., Oxford, 1941–56). Detailed treatment of the drama will be found in Karl Young, *The Drama of the Medieval Church* (2 vols., Oxford, 1933) and F. E. Schelling, *Elizabethan Drama, 1558–1642* (2 vols., Boston, 1908). Hardin Craig, *English Religious Drama of the Middle Ages* (Oxford, 1955) will be serviceable to the specialist rather than to the general reader. A sound and scholarly work is Wilhelm Creizenach, *The English Drama in the Age of Shakespeare* (London, 1916). Brief but useful are F. S. Boas, *An Introduction to Tudor Drama* (Oxford, 1933); C. F. Tucker Brooke, *The Tudor Drama* (Boston,

1911); and F. S. Boas, *An Introduction to Stuart Drama* (Oxford, 1946). E. K. Chambers, *The English Folk-Play* (Oxford, 1933) provides an excellent summary of information on this subject. Informal and readable is W. Bridges-Adams, *The Irresistible Theatre: Vol. I. From the Conquest to the Commonwealth* (London, 1957). Information about the status of actors and the organization of actor-companies may be found in T. W. Baldwin, *The Organization and Personnel of the Shakespearean Company* (Princeton, 1927). A succinct and modern survey of Elizabethan drama is that by Thomas Marc Parrott and Robert H. Ball, *A Short View of Elizabethan Drama* (New York, 1943; paperback edition, 1958).

The most complete history of the Elizabethan theatres is Joseph Q. Adams, *Shakespearean Playhouses: A History of English Theatres from the Beginnings to the Restoration* (Boston, 1917). A useful survey of theatrical history with helpful illustrations is Allardyce Nicoll, *The Development of the Theatre* (London, 1927; New York, 1959). Valuable for its discussion of the English heritage from the classical past is Lily B. Campbell, *Scenes and Machines on the English Stage During the Renaissance: A Classical Revival* (Cambridge, 1923). Valuable information on theatrical practices is available in George F. Reynolds, *The Staging of Elizabethan Plays at the Red Bull Theater, 1605–1625* (New York, 1940). An elaborate discussion of the construction of the Globe theatre will be found in John C. Adams, *The Globe Playhouse: Its Design and Equipment* (Cambridge, Mass., 1942). A model of the Globe made by Mr. Adams and Mr. Irwin Smith is on exhibition in the Folger Library, and a description with scale drawings and pictures is available in Irwin Smith, *Shakespeare's Globe Playhouse: A Modern Reconstruction* (New York, 1956). Another scholar's conception of the construction of the Globe is C. Walter Hodges, *The Globe Restored: A Study of the Elizabethan Theatre* (London, 1953). Students interested in the practical aspects of staging a play on an Elizabethan type of stage will find helpful Richard Southern, *The Open Stage and the Modern Theatre in Research and Practice* (London, 1953).

The literature on the physical aspects of the Elizabethan theatres and the influence of structural features on the drama is extensive and some of it is controversial. An informative book is W. J. Lawrence, *The Physical Conditions of the Elizabethan Public Playhouse* (Cambridge, Mass., 1927). Mr. Lawrence was the author of various articles and monographs giving his views of stage construction. Useful also is Thornton Shirley Graves, *The Court and the London Theatres During the Reign of Queen Elizabeth* (Menasha, Wis., 1913). Collateral information is available in Alfred Harbage, *Shakespeare's Audience* (New York, 1941); Arthur C. Sprague, *Shakespeare and the Audience* (Cambridge, Mass., 1935) and *Shakespearian Players and Performances* (Cambridge, Mass., 1953). Further bibliographical clues to a study of the theatres are available in Allardyce Nicoll, "Studies in the Elizabethan Stage Since 1900," *Shakespeare Survey I* (1948), 1–16.

Christopher Marlowe has been the subject of a number of books in recent years. The new interest in Marlowe began with Leslie Hotson, *The Death of Christopher Marlowe* (London, 1925). The most exhaustive treatment is John Bakeless, *The Tragicall History of Christopher Marlowe* (2 vols., Cambridge, Mass., 1942). Other useful studies include: Frederick S. Boas, *Christopher Marlowe: A Biographical and Critical Study* (Oxford, 1940); Paul H. Kocher, *Christopher Marlowe: A Study of His Thought, Learning, and Character* (Chapel Hill, N. C., 1947); F. P. Wilson, *Marlowe and the Early Shakespeare* (Oxford, 1953); Una M. Ellis-Fermor, *Chris-*

topher Marlowe (London, 1927); Michel Poirier, *Christopher Marlowe* (London, 1951); and C. F. Tucker Brooke, *The Life of Marlowe* (New York, 1930). Editions include: C. F. Tucker Brooke (ed.), *The Works of Christopher Marlowe* (Oxford, 1910); R. H. Case (gen. ed.), *The Works and Life of Christopher Marlowe* (5 vols., New York, 1930–32). The text of *Doctor Faustus* edited by Frederick S. Boas, in the Case edition, is based on the 1616 quarto.

THE TRAGEDY OF

DOCTOR
FAUSTUS

Dramatis Personae

John Faustus, doctor of theology.

Valdes,
Cornelius, } magicians, friends to *Faustus*.

Three Scholars, friends to *Faustus*.

An Old Man.

The Pope.

The Cardinal of Lorraine.

Charles V, Emperor of the Holy Roman Empire.

A Knight.

The Duke of Vanholt.

The Duchess of Vanholt.

A Good Angel.

An Evil Angel.

Mephistophilis.

Lucifer.

Belzebub.

The Seven Deadly Sins,
Alexander the Great,
The Paramour of *Alexander* } spirits.
Helen of Troy,

1

Wagner, servant to *Faustus.*
A Clown.
Robin, an ostler.
Ralph, a servingman.
A Vintner.
A Horse-Courser.
Chorus.
Friars, Devils, Attendants.

The planet Mars with symbols for Scorpio and Taurus.
From *Albumasar de magnis iunctionis* (1515).

Chor. 1. Thrasymene: Lake Trasimene, where Hannibal of Carthage defeated the Romans in 217 B.C. The whole passage probably refers to an heroic play performed by the dramatic company that first put on *Doctor Faustus.*

3. Mars: the Roman god of war; **mate:** checkmate. Marlowe overlooked the fact that the Carthaginians won the battle; **Carthaginians:** inhabitants of Carthage on the North African coast, ancient enemies of Rome.

5. state: the established authority.

7. vaunt: display with pride; the 1616 reading.

10. appeal our plaud: submit for applause.

13. Rhodes: Roda in Saxe-Altenburg.

14. Wittenberg: a famous university town.

15. Whereas: whereat.

THE TRAGEDY OF

Doctor Faustus

Enter *Chorus*.

   Chor. Not marching now in fields of Thrasy-
     mene
Where Mars did mate the Carthaginians,
Nor sporting in the dalliance of love
In courts of kings where state is overturned,   5
Nor in the pomp of proud audacious deeds
Intends our Muse to vaunt his heavenly verse:
Only this, Gentlemen, we must perform,
The form of Faustus' fortunes good or bad.
To patient judgments we appeal our plaud   10
And speak for Faustus in his infancy.
Now is he born, his parents base of stock,
In Germany within a town called Rhodes;
Of riper years to Wittenberg he went
Whereas his kinsmen chiefly brought him up;   15
So soon he profits in divinity,

Icarus.
From Andrea Alciati, *Emblemata* (1583)

17. **scholarism:** scholarship.

21. **cunning:** expert knowledge.

22. **waxen wings:** i.e., the waxen wings contrived by Daedalus for his son, Icarus. The boy ignored his father's warning not to fly too near the sun, his wings melted from his body, and he plummeted to death in the sea.

26. **necromancy:** magic of a sort particularly concerned with divination and communication with the dead.

The fruitful plot of scholarism graced,
That shortly he was graced with Doctor's name,
Excelling all whose sweet delight disputes
In heavenly matters of theology,   20
Till swollen with cunning, of a self-conceit,
His waxen wings did mount above his reach
And melting heavens conspired his overthrow.
For, falling to a devilish exercise,
And glutted more with learning's golden gifts,   25
He surfeits upon cursed necromancy.
Nothing so sweet as magic is to him,
Which he prefers before his chiefest bliss—
And this the man that in his study sits.

Exit.

Aristotle.
From Jean de Tournes,
*Insignium aliquot virorum
icones* (1559).

[I.] 2. sound the depth of that thou wilt profess: get to the bottom of what you will make your specialty.

3. commenced: graduated, not started.

4. level: aim.

6. Analytics: both Aristotle and Marlowe's contemporary Pierre de La Ramée wrote works on this subject.

7. Bene disserere est finis logicis: translated in the succeeding line in question form.

12. on cai me on: Aristotle's phrase for "being and not being," used here as the equivalent of philosophy; **Galen:** a Greek physician and medical writer of the second century A.D.

13. ubi desinit philosophus, ibi incipit medicus: where stops the philosopher, there begins the physician.

16. eternized: made famous forever.

17. Summum bonum medicinae sanitas: health is the greatest benefit of medicine.

[SCENE I]

Enter *Faustus* in his Study.

Faust. Settle thy studies, Faustus, and begin
To sound the depth of that thou wilt profess.
Having commenced, be a divine in show,
Yet level at the end of every art
And live and die in Aristotle's works: 5
Sweet Analytics, 'tis thou hast ravished me!
> [*Reads.*]

Bene disserere est finis logicis—
Is to dispute well logic's chiefest end?
Affords this art no greater miracle?
Then read no more; thou hast attained the end.   10
A greater subject fitteth Faustus' wit:
Bid *on cai me on* farewell, Galen come,
Seeing *ubi desinit philosophus, ibi incipit medi-
cus;*
Be a physician, Faustus, heap up gold   15
And be eternized for some wondrous cure.
> [*Reads.*]

Summum bonum medicinae sanitas—
The end of physic is our bodies' health:
Why, Faustus, hast thou not attained that end?

3

20. **aphorisms:** medical precepts tersely expressed.

21. **bills:** prescriptions.

28. **Justinian:** Byzantine emperor, 483–556 A.D., who ordered the codification of the law.

29-30. **Si una eademque res legatur duobus,/ Alter rem, alter valorem rei:** if the same thing is left to two persons, one shall have the thing itself, the other shall have the value of the thing.

32. **Exhaereditare filium non potest pater nisi:** a father is not able to disinherit his son unless.

33. **the Institute:** an introductory treatise to Justinian's laws.

35. **His:** its; the law's.

36. **external trash:** material wealth.

37. **illiberal:** base (because unconnected with the liberal arts).

39. **Jerome's Bible:** the Bible translated into Latin by St. Jerome, known as the Vulgate.

40. **Stipendium peccati mors est:** the wages of sin is death.

43-4. **Si pecasse negamus, fallimur, et nulla est in nobis veritas:** translated in the lines immediately following.

Is not thy common talk sound aphorisms?   20
Are not thy bills hung up as monuments,
Whereby whole cities have escaped the plague
And thousand desperate maladies been eased?
Yet art thou still but Faustus, and a man.
Couldst thou make men to live eternally   25
Or, being dead, raise them to life again,
Then this profession were to be esteemed.
Physic, farewell. Where is Justinian?   [*Reads.*]
Si una eademque res legatur duobus,
Alter rem, alter valorem rei, etc.—   30
A pretty case of paltry legacies!
Exhaereditare filium non potest pater nisi—
Such is the subject of the Institute
And universal body of the law.
His study fits a mercenary drudge   35
Who aims at nothing but external trash,
Too servile and illiberal for me.
When all is done, divinity is best.
Jerome's Bible, Faustus, view it well: [*Reads.*]
Stipendium peccati mors est—Ha! *Stipendium,*   40
     etc.
The reward of sin is death. That's hard.
Si pecasse negamus, fallimur, et nulla est in nobis
     veritas—
If we say that we have no sin   45
We deceive ourselves, and there's no truth in us.

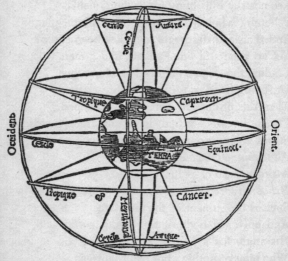

The pole Antartique.

Chart of the earth's place in the cosmos.
From Christopher Cattaneo, *Geomancie* (1591).

47. **belike:** most likely.

52. **metaphysics:** supernatural principles.

59. **quiet poles:** stationary points between which the whole universe revolved.

Why then belike
We must sin and so consequently die,
Ay, we must die an everlasting death.
What doctrine call you this, *Che sera, sera:*   50
What will be, shall be? Divinity, adieu!
These metaphysics of magicians
And necromantic books are heavenly:
Lines, circles, signs, letters and characters—
Ay, these are those that Faustus most desires.   55
O what a world of profit and delight,
Of power, of honor, of omnipotence,
Is promised to the studious artisan!
All things that move between the quiet poles
Shall be at my command. Emperors and kings   60
Are but obeyed in their several provinces,
Nor can they raise the wind or rend the clouds;
But his dominion that exceeds in this
Stretcheth as far as doth the mind of man.
A sound magician is a mighty god: 65
Here, Faustus, try thy brains to gain a deity!

Enter *Wagner.*

Wagner, commend me to my dearest friends,
The German Valdes and Cornelius;
Request them earnestly to visit me.
    Wag. I will, sir.   *Exit.*   70

A scholar in his study.
From Hartmann Schopper, *Panoplia omnium illiberalium* (1568).

82. **glutted with conceit of this:** overwhelmed with this notion.

87. **orient:** lustrous.

Faust. Their conference will be a greater help
    to me
Than all my labors, plod I ne'er so fast.

Enter the *Good Angel* and the *Evil Angel.*

G. Ang. O Faustus, lay that damned book aside
And gaze not on it, lest it tempt thy soul   75
And heap God's heavy wrath upon thy head.
Read, read the Scriptures! That is blasphemy.
E. Ang. Go forward, Faustus, in that famous art
Wherein all nature's treasury is contained:
Be thou on earth, as Jove is in the sky,   80
Lord and commander of these elements.
                              Exeunt Angels.
Faust. How am I glutted with conceit of this!
Shall I make spirits fetch me what I please,
Resolve me of all ambiguities,
Perform what desperate enterprise I will?   85
I'll have them fly to India for gold,
Ransack the ocean for orient pearl,
And search all corners of the new-found world
For pleasant fruits and princely delicates;
I'll have them read me strange philosophy   90
And tell the secrets of all foreign kings;
I'll have them wall all Germany with brass
And make swift Rhine circle fair Wittenberg;

94. **public schools:** universities.

95. **bravely:** splendidly.

97. **Prince of Parma:** Alessandro Farnese, duke of Parma, governor of the Low Countries under Philip II of Spain.

99. **engines:** machines.

100. **the fiery keel at Antwerp's bridge:** a fire ship sent against the bridge during the siege of Antwerp in 1585.

107. **fantasy:** fancy.

108. **receive no object for my head:** dwell on nothing else.

116. **concise syllogisms:** logical reasonings.

117. **Graveled:** perplexed.

I'll have them fill the public schools with silk
Wherewith the students shall be bravely clad;   95
I'll levy soldiers with the coin they bring,
And chase the Prince of Parma from our land
And reign sole king of all our provinces;
Yea, stranger engines for the brunt of war
Than was the fiery keel at Antwerp's bridge   100
I'll make my servile spirits to invent!

Enter Valdes and Cornelius.

Come, German Valdes and Cornelius,
And make me blest with your sage conference.
Valdes, sweet Valdes and Cornelius,
Know that your words have won me at the last 105
To practice magic and concealed arts;
Yet not your words only, but mine own fantasy,
That will receive no object for my head
But ruminates on necromantic skill.
Philosophy is odious and obscure;   110
Both law and physic are for petty wits;
Divinity is basest of the three,
Unpleasant, harsh, contemptible and vile:
'Tis magic, magic, that hath ravished me!
Then, gentle friends, aid me in this attempt,   115
And I that have with concise syllogisms
Graveled the pastors of the German church,

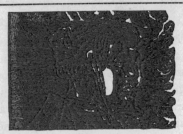

Agrippa.

From *Henry Cornelius Agrippa von Nettesheim. His Fourth Book of Occult Philosophy* (1655).

119. problems: lectures.

120. Musaeus: a mythical poet sometimes confused with Orpheus.

121. Agrippa: Henry Cornelius Agrippa von Nettesheim, 1486–1535, who wrote on occult subjects and had a reputation as a magician.

122. shadows: apparitions.

126. Moors: an Elizabethan generic term for dark-skinned people.

127. subjects of every element: the Elizabethans believed that the cosmos was composed of four cardinal elements: earth, air, fire, and water.

130. Almain rutters: German horsemen; **staves:** spears.

134. queen of love: Venus.

135. argosies: fleets of merchantmen.

137. Philip: King Philip II of Spain.

140. object it not: make no argument about it.

And made the flowering pride of Wittenberg
Swarm to my problems as the infernal spirits
On sweet Musaeus when he came to hell,   120
Will be as cunning as Agrippa was,
Whose shadows made all Europe honor him.
      Vald. Faustus, these books, thy wit, and our
            experience,
Shall make all nations to canonize us.   125
As Indian Moors obey their Spanish lords,
So shall the subjects of every element
Be always serviceable to us three:
Like lions shall they guard us when we please,
Like Almain rutters with their horsemen's staves, 130
Or Lapland giants trotting by our sides;
Sometimes like women, or unwedded maids,
Shadowing more beauty in their airy brows
Than has the white breasts of the queen of love;
From Venice shall they drag huge argosies,   135
And from America the golden fleece
That yearly stuffs old Philip's treasury,
If learned Faustus will be resolute.
      Faust. Valdes, as resolute am I in this
As thou to live; therefore object it not.   140
      Corn. The miracles that magic will perform
Will make thee vow to study nothing else.
He that is grounded in astrology,

Scholars in their study.
From J. Boissard, *Icones quinquaginta virorum* (1597).

144. **well seen:** well equipped, learned.

148. **Delphian oracle:** the oracle of Apollo at Delphi.

152. **massy:** immense.

157. **lusty:** pleasant.

160. **Bacon:** Roger Bacon, 1214–94, who was reputed to be a magician; **Albanus:** probably Pietro d'Abano, 1250–c.1316, an authority on alchemy.

Enriched with tongues, well seen in minerals,
Hath all the principles magic doth require.   145
Then doubt not, Faustus, but to be renowned
And more frequented for this mystery
Than heretofore the Delphian oracle.
The spirits tell me they can dry the sea
And fetch the treasure of all foreign wrecks—   150
Ay, all the wealth that our forefathers hid
Within the massy entrails of the earth.
Then tell me, Faustus, what shall we three want?
 Faust. Nothing, Cornelius. O this cheers my
  soul!   155
Come, show me some demonstrations magical,
That I may conjure in some lusty grove
And have these joys in full possession.
 Vald. Then haste thee to some solitary grove
And bear wise Bacon's and Albanus' works,   160
The Hebrew Psalter and New Testament;
And whatsoever else is requisite
We will inform thee ere our conference cease.
 Corn. Valdes, first let him know the words of
  art,   165
And then, all other ceremonies learned,
Faustus may try his cunning by himself.
 Vald. First I'll instruct thee in the rudiments,
And then wilt thou be perfecter than I.

Galen attending a sick man.
From *Omnia quae extant opera* (1565).
(See [I.] 12.)

172. quiddity: trifling nicety.

Faust. Then come and dine with me, and after 170
  meat
We'll canvas every quiddity thereof;
For ere I sleep I'll try what I can do:
This night I'll conjure though I die therefore.

                                 Exeunt.

[II.] 2-3. **sic probo:** thus I prove it; the formal conclusion of a philosophical argument.

13. **licentiate:** the holder of an undergraduate degree.

[SCENE II]

Enter two *Scholars*.

1. Sch. I wonder what's become of Faustus, that was wont to make our schools ring with *sic probo?*

2. Sch. That shall we know, for see here comes his boy.   5

Enter *Wagner* [carrying wine].

1. Sch. How now, sirrah; where's thy master?

Wag. God in heaven knows.

2. Sch. Why, dost not thou know?

Wag. Yes, I know; but that follows not.

1. Sch. Go to, sirrah; leave your jesting and tell   10
us where he is.

Wag. That follows not necessary by force of argument that you, being licentiate, should stand upon it; therefore acknowledge your error and be attentive.   15

2. Sch. Why, didst thou not say thou knewest?

18. **Ask my fellow if I be a thief:** a proverbial phrase; two of a kind will naturally vouch for each other.

22. **corpus naturale:** a natural body.

23. **mobile:** movable.

27. **place of execution:** scene of action; i.e., the dining room.

29. **sessions:** court sessions.

30. **precisian:** Puritan.

1. Sch. Yes, sirrah, I heard you.

Wag. Ask my fellow if I be a thief.

2. Sch. Well, you will not tell us?

Wag. Yes, sir, I will tell you. Yet if you were 20
not dunces you would never ask me such a question, for is not he *corpus naturale*, and is not that
mobile? Then wherefore should you ask me such
a question? But that I am by nature phlegmatic,
slow to wrath and prone to lechery (to love, I 25
would say), it were not for you to come within
forty foot of the place of execution, although I
do not doubt to see you both hanged the next
sessions. Thus having triumphed over you, I will
set my countenance like a precisian, and begin 30
to speak thus: Truly, my dear brethren, my master is within at dinner with Valdes and Cornelius,
as this wine, if it could speak, it would inform
your worships; and so the Lord bless you, pre-
serve you, and keep you, my dear brethren, my 35
dear brethren.   *Exit.*

1. Sch. Nay, then I fear he is fallen into that
damned art for which they two are infamous
through the world.

2. Sch. Were he a stranger and not allied to 40
me, yet should I grieve for him. But come, let us

42. **Rector:** nominal head of the university.

go and inform the Rector, and see if he by his grave counsel can reclaim him.

1. Sch. O but I fear me nothing can reclaim him. 45

2. Sch. Yet let us try what we can do.

Exeunt.

[III.] 3. **Orion's drizzling look:** the appearance of the constellation Orion was associated with wet weather.

5. **welkin:** heavens.

7. **hest:** behest, command.

10. **anagrammatized:** that is, Faustus has written the tetragrammaton symbolizing the name of God in the pattern of a cross, the letters differently transposed in various directions.

13. **characters of signs:** that is, symbols for the signs of the Zodiac; **erring stars:** planets; **erring** means wandering.

17-21. **Sint . . . Mephistophilis:** grant me your favor, gods of Acheron! Let the triple name of Jehovah prevail! Hail spirits of fire, air, and water! Belzebub, prince of the East, monarch of the fires of hell and, Demogorgon, we propitiate you that Mephistophilis may rise up and appear.

[SCENE III]

Enter *Faustus* to conjure.

Faust. Now that the gloomy shadow of the
    earth,
Longing to view Orion's drizzling look,
Leaps from the antarctic world unto the sky
And dims the welkin with her pitchy breath,   5
Faustus, begin thine incantations,
And try if devils will obey thy hest,
Seeing thou has prayed and sacrificed to them.
       [*He draws a circle on the ground.*]
Within this circle is Jehovah's name
Forward and backward anagrammatized,   10
The 'breviated names of holy saints,
Figures of every adjunct to the heavens,
And characters of signs and erring stars,
By which the spirits are enforced to rise.
Then fear not, Faustus, but be resolute,   15
And try the uttermost magic can perform.
             [*Thunder.*]
*Sint mihi dei Acherontis propitii! Valeat numen
triplex Iehovae! Ignei aerii aquatici spiritus, sal-
vete! Orientis princeps Belzebub, inferni ardentis*

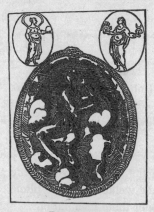

Demogorgon.

From Vincenzo Cartari, *Imagini de gli dei delli antichi* (1615).

20. **Demogorgon:** a primitive god in classical mythology.

22-5. **Quid . . . Mephistophilis:** why do you wait? By Jehovah, by Gehenna, and by the holy water which now I sprinkle, and by the sign of the cross which now I make, and by our prayer, now summoned by us, Mephistophilis, arise!

30. **virtue:** power, as well as the usual meaning.

35. **laureate:** laurel-crowned, analogous to poet laureate.

37. **Quin regis Mephistophilis fratris imagine:** indeed thou rule, Mephistophilis, in the likeness of a friar.

monarcha, et Demogorgon, propitiamus vos, ut   20
appareat et surgat Mephistophilis!

                    [*Faustus pauses. Thunder still.*]
Quid tu moraris? Per Iehovam, Gehennam et con-
secratam aquam quam nunc spargo, signumque
crucis quod nunc facio, et per vota nostra, ipse
nunc surgat nobis dicatus Mephistophilis!   25

                    Enter a *Devil.*

I charge thee to return and change thy shape;
Thou art too ugly to attend on me.
Go, and return an old Franciscan friar;
That holy shape becomes a devil best.
                              Exit Devil.
I see there's virtue in my heavenly words: 30
Who would not be proficient in this art?
How pliant is this Mephistophilis,
Full of obedience and humility!
Such is the force of magic and my spells.
Now, Faustus, thou art conjuror laureate   35
That canst command great Mephistophilis:
Quin regis Mephistophilis fratris imagine!

          Enter *Mephistophilis* [like a *Friar*].

   Meph. Now, Faustus, what wouldst thou have
me do?

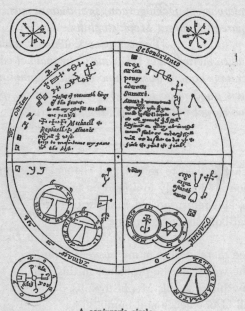

A conjuror's circle.
From *The Book of Magic* (c. 1580). Folger MS. V.b.26
(See [III.] 9.)

53. **per accidens:** that is, not because of Faustus'
power as a conjuror.

54. **rack:** torture, distort; i.e., by anagrammatiz-
ing it.

Faust. I charge thee wait upon me whilst I live   40
To do whatever Faustus shall command,
Be it to make the moon drop from her sphere
Or the ocean to overwhelm the world.

Meph. I am a servant to great Lucifer
And may not follow thee without his leave: 45
No more than he commands must we perform.

Faust. Did not he charge thee to appear to me?

Meph. No, I came now hither of mine own
accord.

Faust. Did not my conjuring speeches raise   50
    thee?
Speak!

Meph. That was the cause, but yet *per accidens,*
For when we hear one rack the name of God,
Abjure the Scriptures and his Saviour Christ,   55
We fly in hope to get his glorious soul;
Nor will we come unless he use such means
Whereby he is in danger to be damned;
Therefore the shortest cut for conjuring
Is stoutly to abjure the Trinity   60
And pray devoutly to the prince of hell.

Faust. So Faustus hath
Already done, and holds this principle,
There is no chief but only Belzebub,
To whom Faustus doth dedicate himself.   65
This word damnation terrifies not him,

67. confounds hell in Elysium: believes hell is as much of a myth as the pagan paradise Elysium.

For he confounds hell in Elysium;
His ghost be with the old philosophers!
But leaving these vain trifles of men's souls—
Tell me what is that Lucifer thy lord?   70
 Meph. Arch-regent and commander of all
  spirits.
 Faust. Was not that Lucifer an angel once?
 Meph. Yes, Faustus, and most dearly loved of
  God.   75
 Faust. How comes it, then, that he is prince of
  devils?
 Meph. O by aspiring pride and insolence
For which God threw him from the face of
  heaven.   80
 Faust. And what are you that live with Lucifer
 Meph. Unhappy spirits that fell with Lucifer,
Conspired against our God with Lucifer,
And are forever damned with Lucifer.
 Faust. Where are you damned?   85
 Meph. In hell.
 Faust. How comes it, then, that thou art out of
  hell?
 Meph. Why, this is hell, nor am I out of it:
Thinkst thou that I who saw the face of God   90
And tasted the eternal joys of heaven
Am not tormented with ten thousand hells
In being deprived of everlasting bliss?

Death and a scholar.
From Fabio Glissenti, *Discorsi morali . . . contra il dispiacer del morire* (1600).

96-7. **passionate:** regretful.

114. **resolve me:** report to me.

O Faustus, leave these frivolous demands
Which strike a terror to my fainting soul! 95
  Faust. What, is great Mephistophilis so pas-
    sionate
For being deprived of the joys of heaven?
Learn thou of Faustus manly fortitude,
And scorn those joys thou never shalt possess. 100
Go, bear these tidings to great Lucifer:
Seeing Faustus hath incurred eternal death
By desperate thoughts against Jove's deity,
Say he surrenders up to him his soul
So he will spare him four-and-twenty years, 105
Letting him live in all voluptuousness,
Having thee ever to attend on me:
To give me whatsoever I shall ask,
To tell me whatsoever I demand,
To slay mine enemies and aid my friends, 110
And always be obedient to my will.
Go, and return to mighty Lucifer,
And meet me in my study at midnight
And then resolve me of thy master's mind.
  Meph. I will, Faustus. *Exit.* 115
  Faust. Had I as many souls as there be stars
I'd give them all for Mephistophilis!
By him I'll be great emperor of the world,
And make a bridge through the moving air
To pass the ocean with a band of men; 120

121. **hills that bind the Afric shore:** hills on both sides of the Straits of Gibraltar.

122. **continent to:** continuous with.

127. **speculation:** contemplation.

I'll join the hills that bind the Afric shore
And make that country continent to Spain,
And both contributory to my crown;
The Emperor shall not live but by my leave,
Nor any potentate of Germany.　　　　　　125
Now that I have obtained what I desire
I'll live in speculation of this art
Till Mephistophilis return again.

Exit.

[IV.] 2. **Swowns:** abbreviation for "God's wounds," a common oath.

3. **pickadevaunts:** beards trimmed to a sharp point.

4. **quotha:** "says he," indeed.

5. **comings in:** income.

9-10. **out of service:** out of a job.

19. **go like:** appear as; **Qui mihi discipulus:** my student.

21. **beaten:** embroidered; **stavesacre:** larkspur seed used in a preparation to kill lice.

[SCENE IV]

Enter *Wagner* and the *Clown*.

Wag. Sirrah boy, come hither.

Clown. How, boy? Swowns, boy! I hope you
have seen many boys with such pickadevaunts
as I have. Boy, quotha!

Wag. Tell me, sirrah, hast thou any comings in?   5

Clown. Ay, and goings out too; you may see
else.

Wag. Alas, poor slave. See how poverty jesteth
in his nakedness: the villain is bare and out of
service, and so hungry that I know he would   10
give his soul to the Devil for a shoulder of mutton, though it were blood-raw.

Clown. How, my soul to the Devil for a
shoulder of mutton, though it were blood-raw?
Not so, good friend: by'r Lady, I had need have   15
it well roasted, and good sauce to it, if I pay so
dear.

Wag. Well, wilt thou serve me, and I'll make
thee go like *Qui mihi discipulus?*

Clown. How, in verse?   20

Wag. No, sirrah, in beaten silk and stavesacre.

20

22. **Knave's Acre:** a low-class area of London now encompassed in Pulteney Street, Soho.

31. **familiars:** evil spirits attached to a particular person.

38. **guilders:** Dutch florins.

40. **crowns:** coins, also bald heads from venereal disease.

41. **Mass:** by the Mass, an oath.

43. **counters:** tokens used by merchants.

Clown. How, how: Knave's Acre? Ay, I thought that was all the land his father left him. Do ye hear, I would be sorry to rob you of your living.

Wag. Sirrah, I say in stavesacre. 25

Clown. Oho, oho: stavesacre! Why then, belike, if I were your man I should be full of vermin.

Wag. So thou shalt, whether thou beest with me or no. But sirrah, leave your jesting, and bind yourself presently unto me for seven years, or I'll 30 turn all the lice about thee into familiars, and they shall tear thee in pieces.

Clown. Do you hear, sir? You may save that labor; they are too familiar with me already. Swowns, they are as bold with my flesh, as if 35 they had paid for my meat and drink.

Wag. Well, do you hear, sirrah?—hold, take these guilders. [*Gives money.*]

Clown. Gridirons—what be they?

Wag. Why, French crowns. 40

Clown. Mass, but for the name of French crowns a man were as good have as many English counters. And what should I do with these?

Wag. Why now, sirrah, thou art at an hour's warning whensoever or wheresoever the Devil 45 shall fetch thee.

Clown. No, no! Here, take your gridirons again.

Wag. Truly, I'll none of them.

A demon.
From Lycosthenus, *Prodigiorum* (1557).

53. **Baliol:** i.e., Belial, a devil.

58. **round slop:** breeches cut in a round, loose shape.

66. **clifts:** clefts.

69. **Banios:** i.e., bagnios, brothels.

Clown. Truly, but you shall.

Wag. Bear witness, I gave them him.   50

Clown. Bear witness, I give them you again.

Wag. Well, I will cause two devils presently to
fetch thee away. Baliol and Belcher! [*Conjures.*]

Clown. Let your Belly-oh and your Belcher
come here, and I'll knock them, they were never   55
so knocked since they were devils. Say I should
kill one of them, what would folks say: "Do ye
see yonder tall fellow in the round slop? He has
killed the Devil!" So I should be called kill-devil
all the parish over.   60

Enter two *Devils,* and the *Clown* runs up and
down crying.

Wag. Baliol and Belcher! Spirits away!

                    Exeunt [*Devils*].

Clown. What, are they gone? A vengeance on
them, they have vile long nails! There was a he-
devil, and a she-devil. I'll tell you how you shall
know them: all he-devils has horns, and all she-   65
devils has clifts and cloven feet.

Wag. Well, sirrah, follow me.

Clown. But do you hear, if I should serve you,
would you teach me to raise up Banios and Bel-
cheos?   70

79. **plackets:** openings in petticoats.

87. **quasi vestigias nostras insistere:** as if treading in my tracks.

89. **fustian:** nonsense.

Wag. I will teach thee to turn thyself to anything—to a dog, or a cat, or a mouse, or a rat, or
anything.

Clown. How? a Christian fellow to a dog or a
cat, a mouse or a rat? No, no, sir! If you turn me   75
into anything, let it be in the likeness of a little
pretty frisking flea, that I may be here and there
and everywhere. O I'll tickle the pretty wenches'
plackets, I'll be amongst them, i'faith!

Wag. Well, sirrah, come.   80

Clown. But do you hear, Wagner?

Wag. How? Baliol and Belcher!

Clown. O Lord, I pray sir, let Banio and
Belcher go sleep.

Wag. Villain, call me Master Wagner, and let   85
thy left eye be diametrally fixt upon my right heel
with *quasi vestigias nostras insistere*.   *Exit.*

Clown. God forgive me, he speaks Dutch
fustian. Well, I'll follow him, I'll serve him; that's
flat.   90

    Exit.

[V.] 4. boots: avails.

[SCENE V]

Enter *Faustus* in his Study.

Faust. Now, Faustus, must thou needs be
    damned
And canst thou not be saved.
What boots it, then, to think of God or heaven?
Away with such vain fancies, and despair—   5
Despair in God and trust in Belzebub.
Now go not backward, no!
Faustus, be resolute: why waverest thou?
O something soundeth in mine ears:
"Abjure this magic, turn to God again!"   10
Ay, and Faustus will turn to God again.
To God? He loves thee not;
The God thou servest is thine own appetite,
Wherein is fixed the love of Belzebub.
To him I'll build an altar and a church   15
And offer lukewarm blood of newborn babes.

Enter *Good Angel* and *Evil Angel*.

G. Ang. Sweet Faustus, leave that execrable art.
E. Ang. Go forward, Faustus, in that famous
    art.

24

31. **seigniory:** proprietorship; **Emden:** a wealthy German seaport.

37. **Veni:** come.

Faust. Contrition, prayer, repentance—what of 20
them?

G. Ang. O they are means to bring thee unto
heaven!

E. Ang. Rather illusions, fruits of lunacy,
That makes men foolish that do trust them most. 25

G. Ang. Sweet Faustus, think of heaven and
heavenly things.

E. Ang. No, Faustus, think of honor and of
wealth. [*Exeunt Angels.*]

Faust. Of wealth! 30
Why, the seigniory of Emden shall be mine.
When Mephistophilis shall stand by me
What God can hurt me? Faustus, thou art safe;
Cast no more doubts. Come, Mephistophilis,
And bring glad tidings from great Lucifer. 35
Is't not midnight? Come, Mephistophilis!
Veni, veni, Mephistophile!

Enter *Mephistophilis.*

Now tell me what says Lucifer, thy lord?

Meph. That I shall wait on Faustus whilst he
lives, 40
So he will buy my service with his soul.

Faust. Already Faustus hath hazarded that for
thee.

45. **solemnly:** formally.

55. **Solamen miseris socios habuisse doloris:** misery loves company.

Meph. But, Faustus, thou must bequeath it
    solemnly   45
And write a deed of gift with thine own blood,
For that security craves great Lucifer.
If thou deny it, I will back to hell.
    Faust. Stay, Mephistophilis, and tell me, what
      good   50
Will my soul do thy lord?
    Meph. Enlarge his kingdom.
    Faust. Is that the reason why he tempts us
      thus?
    Meph. Solamen miseris socios habuisse doloris. 55
    Faust. Why, have you any pain that tortures
      others?
    Meph. As great as have the human souls of
      men.
But tell me, Faustus, shall I have thy soul?   60
And I will be thy slave, and wait on thee,
And tell thee more than thou hast wit to ask.
    Faust. Ay, Mephistophilis, I give it thee.
    Meph. Then, Faustus, stab thine arm coura-
      geously,   65
And bind thy soul that at some certain day
Great Lucifer may claim it as his own,
And then be thou as great as Lucifer.
    Faust. Lo, Mephistophilis, for love of thee
                    [Stabbing his arm]

70. **proper:** own.
80. **straight:** immediately.
S.D. after l. 90. **chafer:** brazier.

I cut mine arm, and with my proper blood   70
Assure my soul to be great Lucifer's.
Chief lord and regent of perpetual night,
View here the blood that trickles from mine arm
And let it be propitious for my wish!
   Meph. But, Faustus, thou must   75
Write it in manner of a deed of gift.
   Faust. Ay, so I will. [*Writes.*] But Mephi-
     stophilis,
My blood congeals and I can write no more.
   Meph. I'll fetch thee fire to dissolve it straight.   80
                             Exit.
   Faust. What might the staying of my blood
     portend?
Is it unwilling I should write this bill?
Why streams it not, that I may write afresh?
"Faustus gives to thee his soul"—ah, there it   85
     stayed.
Why shouldst thou not? Is not thy soul thine
     own?
Then write again: "Faustus gives to thee his
     soul."   90

[Re-]enter *Mephistophilis* with a chafer of coals.

   Meph. Here's fire; come, Faustus, set it on.

A devil.
From Francesco Guazzo, *Compendium maleficarum* (reprint, 1929).

96. **Consummatum est:** it is completed.
99. **Homo, fuge:** flee, Man.

Faust. So: now the blood begins to clear again;
Now will I make an end immediately.   [*Writes.*]
  Meph. [*Aside*] O what will not I do to obtain
    his soul!   95
Faust. Consummatum est—this bill is ended,
And Faustus hath bequeathed his soul to Lucifer.
But what is this inscription on mine arm?
"*Homo, fuge!*" Whither should I fly?
If unto God, he'll throw me down to hell.   100
My senses are deceived; here's nothing writ.
I see it plain: here in this place is writ
"*Homo, fuge!*" Yet shall not Faustus fly.
  Meph. I'll fetch him somewhat to delight his
    mind.   *Exit.* 105

[Re-]enter [*Mephistophilis*] with *Devils,* giving
crowns and rich apparel to *Faustus,* and dance,
and then depart.

Faust. Speak, Mephistophilis, what means this
    show?
  Meph. Nothing, Faustus, but to delight thy
    mind withal
And to show thee what magic can perform.   110
  Faust. But may I raise up spirits when I please?
  Meph. Ay, Faustus, and do greater things than
    these.

119. **articles:** agreements.

Faust. Then there's enough for a thousand
    souls. 115
Here, Mephistophilis, receive this scroll,
A deed of gift of body and of soul;
But yet conditionally that thou perform
All articles prescribed between us both.

  Meph. Faustus, I swear by hell and Lucifer 120
To effect all promises between us made.

  Faust. Then hear me read them: [*Reads.*]
"On these conditions following:
First, that Faustus may be a spirit in form and
    substance. 125
Secondly, that Mephistophilis shall be his servant
    and at his command.
Thirdly, that Mephistophilis shall do for him, and
    bring him whatsoever.
Fourthly, that he shall be in his chamber or 130
    house invisible.
Lastly, that he shall appear to the said John
    Faustus at all times, in what form or shape
    soever he please.
I, John Faustus of Wittenberg, Doctor, by these 135
    presents do give both body and soul to
    Lucifer, Prince of the East, and his minister
    Mephistophilis, and furthermore grant unto
    them, that twenty-four years being expired,

140. **inviolate:** unbroken; that is, the contract having been kept.

155. **these elements:** the whole cosmos.

157. **circumscribed:** limited.

158. **self:** particular.

the articles above written inviolate, full 140
power to fetch or carry the said John Faustus
body and soul, flesh, blood, or goods, into
their habitation wheresoever.

By me John Faustus."

Meph. Speak, Faustus, do you deliver this as 145
your deed?

Faust. Ay, take it, and the Devil give thee good
on't.

Meph. Now, Faustus, ask what thou wilt.

Faust. First will I question with thee about hell. 150
Tell me, where is the place that men call hell?

Meph. Under the heavens.

Faust.   Ay, but where-
about?

Meph. Within the bowels of these elements, 155
Where we are tortured and remain forever.
Hell hath no limits, nor is circumscribed
In one self place, for where we are is hell,
And where hell is there must we ever be;
And, to conclude, when all the world dissolves, 160
And every creature shall be purified,
All places shall be hell that is not heaven.

Faust. Come, I think hell's a fable.

Meph. Ay, think so, till experience change thy
mind.   165

171. **fond:** foolish.
178. **and:** if.

Faust. Why, thinkst thou then that Faustus
    shall be damned?

Meph. Ay, of necessity, for here's the scroll
Wherein thou hast given thy soul to Lucifer.

Faust. Ay, and body too; but what of that? 170
Thinkst thou that Faustus is so fond to imagine
That after this life there is any pain?
Tush, these are trifles and mere old wives' tales.

Meph. But, Faustus, I am an instance to prove
    the contrary,   175
For I am damned, and am now in hell.

Faust. How, now in hell?
Nay, and this be hell I'll willingly be damned
    here.
What, walking, disputing, et cetera?   180
But leaving off this, let me have a wife,
The fairest maid in Germany,
For I am wanton and lascivious
And cannot live without a wife.

Meph. How, a wife?   185
I prithee, Faustus, talk not of a wife.

Faust. Nay, sweet Mephistophilis, fetch me one,
for I will have one.

Meph. Well, thou wilt have one. Sit there till
    I come;   190
I'll fetch thee a wife in the Devil's name. [*Exit.*]

Penelope.
From *Promptuarii iconum* (1553).

196. **ceremonial toy:** formal triviality.

198. **cull thee out:** select carefully for you.

202. **Penelope:** the wife of Ulysses, who awaited his return patiently despite the clamors of the suitors anxious to replace him.

203. **Saba:** the Queen of Sheba.

206. **iterating:** repetition.

213-14. **fain would I:** I would like to.

..us,
...... but a ceremonial toy.
.... lovest me, think no more of it.
.. cull thee out the fairest courtesans
And bring them every morning to thy bed;
She whom thine eye shall like thy heart shall   200
    have,
Be she as chaste as was Penelope,
As wise as Saba, or as beautiful
As was bright Lucifer before his fall.
Hold, take this book: peruse it thoroughly.   205
The iterating of these lines brings gold,
The framing of this circle on the ground
Brings whirlwinds, tempests, thunder and light-
    ning;
Pronounce this thrice devoutly to thyself   210
And men in armor shall appear to thee,
Ready to execute what thou desirest.

   Faust. Thanks, Mephistophilis, yet fain would

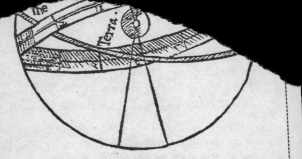

The Zodiac.
From Christopher Cattaneo, *Geomancie* (1591).

219. **characters and planets:** characteristics of the planets.

220. **dispositions:** locations.

I have a book wherein I might behold all sp
and incantations, that I might raise up sp
when I please.

Meph. Here they are in this book.

There tur

Faust. Now would I have a book w
see all characters and planets of
that I might know their motions a

Meph. Here they are too.

Faust. Nay, let me have on
then I have done, wherein I
herbs, and trees that grow

Meph. Here they be.

Faust. O thou art deceived!

Meph. Tut, I warrant thee. *Tur*

[Exeu

SCENE V

32

[Re-]enter [Mephistophilis] with worksessed

like a woman, with

Meph. Tell me, Faustus, how dost thou

thy wife?

Faust. A plague on her for a hot whore!

[Exit Devil.]

Meph. Tut, Faust

Marriage is

If thou

I'll

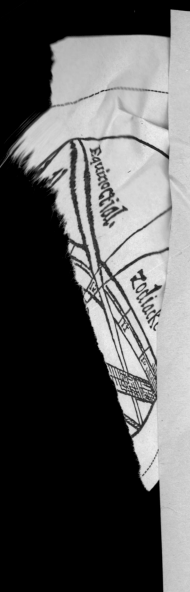

[VI.] 15, yet: that is, even now.

34

Be
Ay,
  E.

  Fa
Scarc
But fe
"Faust
  kn
Poison,
Are laid
And lon
Had not
Have I n
Of Alexan
And hath
With ravis
Made musi
Why should
I am resolve
Come, Meph
And argue o
Tell me, are th
Are all celestia
As is the subst

[SCENE VI]

[Enter Faust in his Study, and Mephistophilis.]

Faust. When I behold the heavens, then I re-
pent
And curse thee, wicked Mephistophilis,
Because thou hast deprived me of those joys.   5
  Meph. Why, Faustus,
Thinkst thou heaven is such a glorious thing?
I tell thee, 'tis not half so fair as thou,
Or any man that breathes on earth.
  Faust. How provest thou that?
  Meph. It was made for man; therefore is man 10
more excellent.
  Faust. If it were made for man 'twas made for
me.
I will renounce this magic and repent.

Enter Good Angel and Evil Angel.

  G. Ang. Faustus, repent; yet God will pity 15
thee.
  E. Ang. Thou art a spirit; God cannot pity
thee.

The planet Saturn.
From *Albumasar de magnis iunctionis* (1515).

47. **axletree:** axis.

50. **erring:** wandering; see [III.] 13.

52. **situ et tempore:** in place and time.

56. **zodiac:** an imaginary belt of the heavens in which are the apparent paths of the sun, the moon, and the principal planets.

67-8. **dominion or Intelligentia:** ruling spirit.

Meph. As are the elements, such are the
    spheres,   45
Mutually folded in each other's orb;
And jointly move upon one axletree
Whose terminine is termed the world's wide pole;
Nor are the names of Saturn, Mars, or Jupiter
Feigned, but are erring stars.   50

Faust. But tell me, have they all one motion,
both *situ et tempore?*

Meph. All jointly move from East to West in
twenty-four hours upon the poles of the world,
but differ in their motion upon the poles of the 55
zodiac.

Faust. Tush, these slender trifles Wagner can
    decide.
Hath Mephistophilis no greater skill?
Who knows not the double motion of the 60
    planets?
The first is finished in a natural day;
The second thus, as Saturn in thirty years, Jupiter
in twelve, Mars in four, the Sun, Venus, and
Mercury in a year, the Moon in twenty-eight 65
days. Tush, these are freshmen's suppositions. But
tell me, hath every sphere a dominion or *In-
telligentia?*

Meph. Ay.

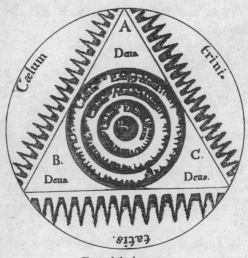

Chart of the heavens.
From Robert Fludd, *Utriusque cosmi maioris et minoris metaphysica* . . . (1617).

74-5. **coelum igneum, et crystallinum**: a burning heaven and a crystalline heaven, parts of the Ptolemaic concept of the universe.

78. **conjunctions, oppositions, etc.**: astrological terms for the positions of the planets.

81. **Per inequalem motum respectu totius**: on account of the unequal motion in relation to the whole.

86. **Move**: urge.

Faust. How many heavens or spheres are   70
there?

Meph. Nine: the seven planets, the firmament,
and the empyreal heaven.

Faust. But is there not *coelum igneum, et
crystallinum?*   75

Meph. No, Faustus, they be but fables.

Faust. Well, resolve me in this question: why
have we not conjunctions, oppositions, aspects,
eclipses, all at one time, but in some years we
have more, in some less?   80

Meph. Per inequalem motum respectu totius.

Faust. Well, I am answered. Tell me, who
made the world?

Meph. I will not.

Faust. Sweet Mephistophilis, tell me.   85

Meph. Move me not, for I will not tell thee.

Faust. Villain, have I not bound thee to tell
me anything?

Meph. Ay, that is not against our kingdom;
but this is.   90
Think thou on hell, Faustus, for thou art damned.

Faust. Think, Faustus, upon God that made
the world!

Meph. Remember this!   *Exit.*

Faust. Ay, go, accursed spirit, to ugly hell;   95

102. raze: cut slightly, graze.

'Tis thou has damned distressed Faustus' soul.
Is't not too late?

Enter *Good Angel* and *Evil Angel*.

E. Ang. Too late.
G. Ang. Never too late, if Faustus can repent.
E. Ang. If thou repent, devils shall tear thee 100
in pieces.
G. Ang. Repent, and they shall never raze thy
    skin.   *Exeunt Angels.*
Faust. Ah Christ, my Saviour!
Seek to save distressed Faustus' soul.   105

Enter *Lucifer, Belzebub,* and *Mephistophilis.*

Luc. Christ cannot save thy soul, for he is just;
There's none but I have interest in the same.
Faust. O who art thou that lookst so terrible?
Luc. I am Lucifer,
And this is my companion prince in hell.   110
Faust. O Faustus, they are come to fetch away
thy soul!
Luc. We come to tell thee thou dost injure us:
Thou callst on Christ, contrary to thy promise.
Thou shouldst not think of God; think of the 115
    Devil,—

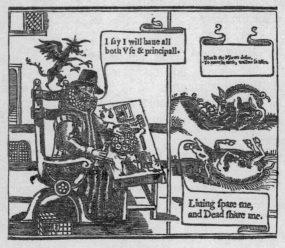

An English usurer.
From John Blaxton, *The English Usurer* (1623).
(See [VI.] 150 ff.)

117. **dam:** mother.
124. **gratify thee:** make it worth your while.

And of his dam too.

Faust. Nor will I henceforth. Pardon me in
  this,
And Faustus vows never to look to heaven,   120
Never to name God or to pray to him,
To burn his Scriptures, slay his ministers,
And make my spirits pull his churches down.

Luc. Do so, and we will highly gratify thee.
Faustus, we are come from hell to show thee some 125
pastime: sit down, and thou shalt see all the
Seven Deadly Sins appear in their proper shapes.

Faust. That sight will be as pleasing unto me
as paradise was to Adam, the first day of his
creation.   130

Luc. Talk not of paradise nor creation, but
mark this show; talk of the Devil and nothing
else. Come, away!

Enter the *Seven Deadly Sins*.

Now, Faustus, examine them of their several
names and dispositions.   135

Faust. What are thou, the first?

Pride. I am Pride. I disdain to have any parents. I am like to Ovid's flea: I can creep into
every corner of a wench; sometimes like a peri-
wig I sit upon her brow; next like a necklace I 140

Furore (Wrath).
From Vincenzo Cartari, *Imagini de gli dei delli antichi* (1615).

143. **wrought smock:** embroidered undergarment; **list:** wish, please.

146. **cloth of arras:** Flemish tapestry.

150. **churl:** miser; **leathern bag:** i.e., moneybag. The implication is that Covetousness was conceived by the first paltry collection of coins a miser gathered.

158. **case:** pair.

hang about her neck, or like a fan of feathers
I kiss her lips; and then turning myself to a
wrought smock do what I list. But fie, what a
scent is here! I'll not speak another word except
the ground were perfumed and covered with 145
cloth of arras.

Faust. Thou art a proud knave indeed. What
art thou, the second?

Covet. I am Covetousness, begotten of an old
churl in an old leathern bag; and, might I have 150
my wish, I would desire that this house and all
the people in it were turned to gold, that I might
lock you up in my chest. O my sweet gold!

Faust. What art thou, the third?

Wrath. I am Wrath. I had neither father nor 155
mother; I leaped out of a lion's mouth when I
was scarce half an hour old, and ever since I have
run up and down the world with this case of
rapiers, wounding myself when I had nobody to
fight withal. I was born in hell; and look to it, 160
for some of you shall be my father.

Faust. What art thou, the fourth?

Envy. I am Envy, begotten of a chimney-
sweeper and an oyster-wife. I cannot read, and
therefore wish all books were burned. I am lean 165
with seeing others eat. O that there would come
a famine through all the world, that all might

Invidia (Envy).
From Vincenzo Cartari, *Imagini de gli dei delli antichi* (1615).

176. **bevers:** snacks.
185. **progeny:** forebears; not offspring.

die, and I live alone; then thou shouldst see how
fat I would be! But must thou sit and I stand?
Come down, with a vengeance!   170

Faust. Away, envious rascal! What art thou,
the fifth?

Glut. Who, I, sir? I am Gluttony. My parents
are all dead, and the devil a penny they have left
me but a bare pension, and that is thirty meals 175
a day and ten bevers—a small trifle to suffice nature. O I come of a royal parentage: my grand-
father was a gammon of bacon, my grandmother
a hogshead of claret wine. My godfathers were
these: Peter Pickle-herring and Martin Martle- 180
mas-beef. O but my godmother—she was a jolly
gentlewoman, and well beloved in every good
town and city: her name was mistress Margery
March-beer. Now, Faustus, thou hast heard all
my progeny; wilt thou bid me to supper?   185

Faust. No, I'll see thee hanged! Thou wilt eat
up all my victuals.

Glut. Then the Devil choke thee.

Faust. Choke thyself, glutton. What art thou,
the sixth?   190

Sloth. I am Sloth. I was begotten on a sunny
bank, where I have lain ever since, and you have
done me great injury to bring me from thence;
let me be carried thither again by Gluttony and

Lascivia (Lechery).
From Andrea Alciati, *Emblemata* (1583).

215. **chary:** safely.

Lechery. I'll not speak another word for a king's 195
ransom.

Faust. What are you, mistress minx, the seventh
and last?

Lech. Who, I, sir? I am one that loves an inch
of raw mutton better than an ell of fried stock- 200
fish, and the first letter of my name begins with
L—echery.

Luc. Away, to hell, to hell!   *Exeunt the Sins.*
Now, Faustus, how dost thou like this?

Faust. O this feeds my soul!   205

Luc. Tut, Faustus, in hell is all manner of
delight.

Faust. O that I might see hell and return
again, how happy were I then!

Luc. Thou shalt. I will send for thee at mid- 210
night. In mean time take this book, peruse it thoroughly, and thou shalt turn thyself into what
shape thou wilt.

Faust. Great thanks, mighty Lucifer;
This will I keep as chary as my life.   215

Luc. Farewell, Faustus, and think on the Devil.

Faust. Farewell, great Lucifer. Come, Mephistophilis.

                              Exeunt omnes.

Gluttony.
From Andrea Alciati, *Emblemata* (1608).
(See [VI.] 173 ff.)

[VII.] Entrance: **solus:** alone.

7. **prove:** test the accuracy of; **cosmography:** study of the universe.

10. **take some part of:** i.e., take part in; **holy Peter's feast:** the celebration of St. Peter's Day.

11. **solemnized:** formally observed.

13. **Trier:** Trèves, on the Moselle River.

[SCENE VII]

Enter *Wagner* solus, as *Chorus.*

Wag. Learned Faustus,
To know the secrets of astronomy
Graven in the book of Jove's high firmament,
Did mount himself to scale Olympus' top,
Being seated in a chariot burning bright   5
Drawn by the strength of yoked dragons' necks:
He now is gone to prove cosmography,
And, as I guess, will first arrive at Rome
To see the Pope and manner of his court,
And take some part of holy Peter's feast,   10
The which this day is highly solemnized.
                                   Exit Wagner.

Enter *Faustus* and *Mephistophilis.*

Faust. Having now, my good Mephistophilis,
Passed with delight the stately town of Trier
Environed round with airy mountain tops,
With walls of flint and deep-entrenched lakes,   15
Not to be won by any conquering prince;

43

Virgil's tomb.
From Francis Misson, *A New Voyage to Italy* (1695).

20. **Campagna:** a region in southern Italy.

25. **Maro:** Virgil; in the Middle Ages he was given the attributes of a magician.

33. **erst:** formerly.

37. **privy:** private.

From Paris next coasting the realm of France,
We saw the river Main fall into Rhine,
Whose banks are set with groves of fruitful vines;
Then up to Naples, rich Campagna, 20
Whose buildings fair and gorgeous to the eye,
The streets straight forth and paved with finest
    brick
Quarters the town in four equivalents.
There saw we learned Maro's golden tomb, 25
The way he cut, an English mile in length,
Thorough a rock of stone in one night's space.
From thence to Venice, Padua, and the rest,
In midst of which a sumptuous temple stands
That threats the stars with her aspiring top. 30
Thus hitherto hath Faustus spent his time.
But tell me now, what resting place is this?
Hast thou, as erst I did command,
Conducted me within the walls of Rome?

    Meph. Faustus, I have; and because we will 35
not be unprovided, I have taken up his Holiness'
privy chamber for our use.

    Faust. I hope his Holiness will bid us wel-
come.

    Meph. Tut, 'tis no matter, man; we'll be bold 40
with his good cheer.
And now, my Faustus, that thou mayst perceive
What Rome containeth to delight thee with,

52. **passing:** exceedingly.

56. **pyramides:** Marlowe evidently refers to the obelisk brought from Egypt by Constantius in the fourth century.

68. **summum bonum:** highest good.

69. **compass:** obtain.

Know that this city stands upon seven hills
That underprops the groundwork of the same;   45
Just through the midst runs flowing Tiber's
     stream,
With winding banks that cut it in two parts,
Over the which four stately bridges lean
That makes safe passage to each part of Rome.   50
Upon the bridge called Ponto Angelo
Erected is a castle passing strong,
Within whose walls such store of ordnance are,
And double cannons framed of carved brass,
As match the days within one complete year—   55
Besides the gates and high pyramides
Which Julius Cæsar brought from Africa.

     Faust. Now by the kingdoms of infernal rule,
Of Styx, Acheron, and the fiery lake
Of ever-burning Phlegethon, I swear   60
That I do long to see the monuments
And situation of bright-splendent Rome.
Come, therefore, let's away.

     Meph. Nay, Faustus, stay; I know you'd fain
     see the Pope   65
And take some part of holy Peter's feast,
Where thou shalt see a troop of bald-pate friars
Whose *summum bonum* is in belly-cheer.

     Faust. Well, I am content to compass then
     some sport   70

Clauaere fiaereas, ac aperire fores.
Regna Sacerdotum mihi pontificalia parent,
Maximus vt Christi Pastor ouile regam.

The Pope.
From Hartmann Schopper, *Panoplia omnium illiberalium* (1568).

S.D. after l. 76. **sennet:** trumpet fanfare.
79. **Fall to:** begin; **and:** if; see [V.] 179.
83. **like:** please.

And by their folly make us merriment.
Then charm me that I may be invisible,
To do what I please
Unseen of any whilst I stay in Rome.

                     [*Mephistophilis gestures.*]

  Meph. So, Faustus; now   75
Do what thou wilt thou shalt not be discerned.

Sound a sennet. Enter the *Pope* and the *Cardinal
of Lorraine* to the banquet, with *Friars* attending.

  Pope. My Lord of Lorraine, will't please you
draw near?
  Faust. Fall to, and the Devil choke you and
you spare.   80
  Pope. How now, who's that which spake?
Friars look about.
  Friar. Here's nobody, if it like your Holiness.
  Pope. My lord, here is a dainty dish was sent
me from the Bishop of Milan.   85
  Faust. I thank you, sir.   *Snatch it.*
  Pope. How now, who's that which snatched
the meat from me? Will no man look? My lord,
this dish was sent me from the Cardinal of Flor-
ence.   90
  Faust. You say true; I'll ha't.   [*Snatch it.*]

A cardinal.
From Hartmann Schopper, *Panoplia omnium illiberalium* (1568).

99. **lay:** suppress.
103. **Aware:** beware.

Pope. What, again! My lord, I'll drink to your grace.

Faust. I'll pledge your grace.　　　　[*Snatch it.*]

Lorr. My Lord, it may be some ghost newly 95
crept out of Purgatory come to beg a pardon of
your Holiness.

Pope. It may be so. Friars, prepare a dirge to
lay the fury of this ghost. Once again, my lord,
fall to.　　　　　　*The Pope crosseth himself.* 100

Faust. What, are you crossing of yourself?
Well, use that trick no more, I would advise you.
　　　　　　　　　　　　Cross again.
Well, that's the second time. Aware the third,
I give you fair warning.

　　　*Cross again, and Faustus hits him a box of
　　　　　　the ear, and they all run away.*

Faust. Come on, Mephistophilis, what shall we 105
do?

Meph. Nay, I know not; we shall be cursed
with bell, book, and candle.

Faust. How! bell, book, and candle, candle,
　　　book, and bell,　　　　　　　　　　　110
Forward and backward to curse Faustus to hell.
Anon you shall hear a hog grunt, a calf bleat,
　　　and an ass bray,
Because it is Saint Peter's holy day.

118. **maledicat dominus:** the Lord curse him.
126. **Et omnes sancti:** and all the saints.

Enter all the *Friars* to sing the dirge.

Friar. Come, brethren, let's about our busi- 115
ness with good devotion.

All sing this:

Cursed be he that stole away his Holiness' meat
 from the table—*maledicat dominus!*
Cursed be he that struck his Holiness a blow
 on the face—*maledicat dominus!*   120
Cursed be he that took Friar Sandelo a blow
 on the pate—*maledicat dominus!*
Cursed be he that disturbeth our holy dirge—
 maledicat dominus!
Cursed be he that took away his Holiness' 125
 wine—*maledicat dominus! Et omnes sancti!*
 Amen.
  Beat the Friars, and fling fireworks among
        them, and so exeunt.

[**VIII.**] 3. **search:** i.e., search out; **circles:** magical formulae.
11. **chafing:** dispute.

[SCENE VIII]

Enter *Robin the Ostler* with a book in his hand.

Rob. O this is admirable! Here I ha' stolen
one of Doctor Faustus' conjuring books, and,
i'faith, I mean to search some circles for my own
use: now will I make all the maidens in our parish dance at my pleasure stark naked before me,   5
and so by that means I shall see more than e'er
I felt or saw yet.

Enter *Ralph* calling *Robin.*

Ralph. Robin, prithee come away, there's a
gentleman tarries to have his horse, and he would
have his things rubbed and made clean. He keeps   10
such a chafing with my mistress about it, and she
has sent me to look thee out; prithee, come away.
Rob. Keep out, keep out, or else you are blown
up, you are dismembered, Ralph; keep out, for
I am about a roaring piece of work.   15
Ralph. Come, what doest thou with that same
book? Thou canst not read.

49

19. **forehead:** Robin boasts that he will seduce his master's wife. The reference is specifically to the horns of the cuckold, as a betrayed husband was called.

28. **ippocras:** hippocras, a spiced sweet wine.

31. **nothing:** i.e., naught, wicked.

Rob. Yes, my master and mistress shall find
that I can read—he for his forehead, she for her
private study. She's born to bear with me, or   20
else my art fails.

Ralph. Why, Robin, what book is that?

Rob. What book? Why the most intolerable
book for conjuring that e'er was invented by any
brimstone devil.   25

Ralph. Canst thou conjure with it?

Rob. I can do all these things easily with it:
first, I can make thee drunk with ippocras at
any tavern in Europe for nothing; that's one of
my conjuring works.   30

Ralph. Our master Parson says that's nothing.

Rob. True, Ralph; and more, Ralph, if thou
hast any mind to Nan Spit our kitchen maid,
then turn her and wind her to thy own use as
often as thou wilt, and at midnight.   35

Ralph. O brave, Robin! Shall I have Nan Spit,
and to mine own use? On that condition I'll feed
thy devil with horse-bread as long as he lives,
of free cost.

Rob. No more, sweet Ralph. Let's go and   40
make clean our boots which lie foul upon our
hands, and then to our conjuring in the Devil's
name.

Exeunt.

[IX.] 2-3. **Ecce signum:** behold the sign.

3. **simple purchase:** small gain.

S.D. after l. 5. **Vintner:** wineseller.

7. **gull:** fool; **supernaturally:** extraordinarily.

8. **Drawer:** one who serves wine and beer in a tavern.

13. **etc.:** this use of et cetera, as often used in Elizabethan drama, suggests that the clown was to interpolate something. Some Elizabethan clowns were famous for their extempore interpolations.

15. **favor:** approval.

[SCENE IX]

Enter *Robin* and *Ralph* with a silver goblet.

Rob. Come, Ralph, did I not tell thee we were forever made by this Doctor Faustus' book? *Ecce signum:* here's a simple purchase for horse-keepers! Our horses shall eat no hay as long as this lasts.   5

Enter the *Vintner*.

Ralph. But Robin, here comes the vintner.

Rob. Hush, I'll gull him supernaturally. Drawer, I hope all is paid; God be with you. Come, Ralph.

Vint. Soft, sir, a word with you: I must yet   10
have a goblet paid from you ere you go.

Rob. I a goblet? Ralph—I a goblet? I scorn you, and you are but a etc. I a goblet? Search me.

Vint. I mean so, sir, with your favor.   15
                              [*Searches Robin.*]

Rob. How say you now?

20-1. **burden honest men with a matter of truth:** challenge the veracity of honest men.

22. **t'one:** one or the other.

24. **afore:** before.

31. **Sanctobulorum Periphrasticon:** a nonsensical parody of a conjuror's incantation.

33-4. **Polypragmos . . . etc.:** further nonsense.

S.D. after l. 34. **squibs:** firecrackers.

35. **nomine Domine:** in the name of God.

37. **Peccatum peccatorum:** Sin of sins.

Vint. I must say somewhat to your fellow:
you, sir.

Ralph. Me, sir, me, sir? Search your fill.

[*Searches Ralph.*]

Now, sir, you may be ashamed to burden honest 20
men with a matter of truth.

Vint. Well, t'one of you hath this goblet about
you.

Rob. [*Aside*] You lie, drawer, 'tis afore me.—
Sirrah you, I'll teach ye to impeach honest men! 25
Stand by: I'll scour you for a goblet; stand aside,
you had best, I charge you in the name of Belzebub. [*Aside*] Look to the goblet, Ralph.

Vint. What mean you, sirrah?

Rob. I'll tell you what I mean: *Reads.* 30
Sanctobulorum Periphrasticon—nay, I'll tickle
you, vintner. [*Aside*] Look to the goblet, Ralph.
*Polypragmos Belseborams framanto pacostiphos
tostu Mephistophilis etc.*

Enter *Mephistophilis*, sets squibs at their backs
       [and withdraws]. They run about.

Vint. O *nomine Domine!* what meanest thou, 35
Robin? Thou hast no goblet.

Ralph. Peccatum peccatorum! here's thy goblet,
good vintner.   [*Exit Vintner, with goblet.*]

39. **Misericordia pro nobis:** Mercy on us.
44. **awful:** full of awe.
55. **brave:** splendid.
57. **enow:** enough.

Rob. Misericordia pro nobis! what shall I do?
Good Devil, forgive me now and I'll never rob 40
thy library more.

[Re-]enter to them *Mephistophilis.*

Meph. Monarch of hell, under whose black
    survey
Great potentates do kneel with awful fear,
Upon whose altars thousand souls do lie, 45
How am I vexed with these villains' charms!
From Constantinople am I hither come
Only for pleasure of these damned slaves.
Rob. How, from Constantinople? You have
had a great journey: will you take sixpence in 50
your purse to pay for your supper, and be gone?
Meph. Well, villains, for your presumption I
transform thee into an ape, and thee into a dog;
and so be gone.   *Exit.*
Rob. How, into an ape? That's brave: I'll have 55
fine sport with the boys; I'll get nuts and apples
enow.
Ralph. And I must be a dog.
Rob. I'faith, thy head will never be out of the
pottage-pot.   60

                                                Exeunt.

[X.] 7. **gratulate:** congratulate.

8. **conference:** conversation.

10. **astrology:** astronomy; see [VI.] 40.

15. **Carolus the Fifth:** Charles V, Emperor of the Holy Roman Empire.

[SCENE X]

Enter *Chorus*.

Chor. When Faustus had with pleasure ta'en
 the view
Of rarest things and royal courts of kings,
He stayed his course and so returned home,
Where such as bear his absence but with grief,   5
I mean his friends and nearest companions,
Did gratulate his safety with kind words,
And in their conference of what befell
Touching his journey through the world and air,
They put forth questions of astrology   10
Which Faustus answered with such learned skill
As they admired and wondered at his wit.
Now is his fame spread forth in every land:
Amongst the rest the Emperor is one,
Carolus the Fifth, at whose palace now   15
Faustus is feasted mongst his noblemen.
What there he did in trial of his art
I leave untold, your eyes shall see performed.

35. **nothing answerable:** in no way comparable.
36. **for that:** because.
41. **set:** seated.

Enter *Emperor, Faustus, Mephistophilis,* and a
Knight, with *Attendants.*

Emp. Master Doctor Faustus, I have heard
strange report of thy knowledge in the black art, 20
how that none in my empire nor in the whole
world can compare with thee for the rare effects
of magic. They say thou hast a familiar spirit, by
whom thou canst accomplish what thou list. This,
therefore, is my request, that thou let me see 25
some proof of thy skill, that mine eyes may be
witnesses to confirm what mine ears have heard
reported; and here I swear to thee, by the honor
of mine imperial crown, that whatever thou doest
thou shalt be no ways prejudiced or endamaged. 30

Kni. [*Aside*] I'faith, he looks much like a conjuror.

Faust. My gracious Sovereign, though I must
confess myself far inferior to the report men
have published, and nothing answerable to the 35
honor of your imperial Majesty, yet for that love
and duty binds me thereunto, I am content to do
whatsoever your majesty shall command me.

Emp. Then, Doctor Faustus, mark what I shall
say: 40
As I was sometime solitary set

Actaeon beset by his hounds.
From Andrea Alciati, *Emblemata* (1583).

42. **closet:** private chamber.

51. **the world's pre-eminence:** those most
famed in the history of the world.

54. **motion:** mention.

59. **paramour:** mistress.

60. **gesture:** general behavior.

Within my closet, sundry thoughts arose
About the honor of mine ancestors—
How they had won by prowess such exploits,
Got such riches, subdued so many kingdoms,   45
As we that do succeed or they that shall
Hereafter possess our throne shall,
I fear me, never attain to that degree
Of high renown and great authority.
Amongst which kings is Alexander the Great,   50
Chief spectacle of the world's pre-eminence,
The bright shining of whose glorious acts
Lightens the world with his reflecting beams,
As when I hear but motion made of him
It grieves my soul I never saw the man.   55
If, therefore, thou by cunning of thine art
Canst raise this man from hollow vaults below
Where lies entombed this famous conqueror,
And bring him with his beauteous paramour,
Both in their right shapes, gesture, and attire   60
They used to wear during their time of life,
Thou shalt both satisfy my just desire
And give me cause to praise thee whilst I live.

   Faust. My gracious Lord, I am ready to accomplish your request, so far forth as by art and   65
power of my spirit I am able to perform.

   Kni. [*Aside*] I'faith, that's just nothing at all.

   Faust. But if it like your Grace, it is not in my

72. **marry:** a mild oath derived from "by the Virgin Mary." Here it means something like "indeed."

73. **grace:** virtue.

75. **lively:** to the life.

81. **Go to:** good enough; you have said all that's necessary by way of introduction. **Go to** is used variously as an exclamation of reproof or impatience.

82. **presently:** at once.

88. **Actaeon:** a hunter who chanced upon Diana bathing and was changed by her to a stag and destroyed by his own hounds.

89. **horns:** Faustus taunts him with being a cuckold; see [VIII.] 19. This was a stock joke and did not necessarily refer to the true state of a man's domestic affairs. Possibly because he was a man who acquired horns, Actaeon's name is often referred to in such jests. The cuckold's horns may derive from some version of Actaeon's story, but the connection is obscure.

91. **meet:** get even.

ability to present before your eyes the true substantial bodies of those two deceased princes   70
which long since are consumed to dust.

Kni. [*Aside*] Ay marry, Master Doctor, now
there's a sign of grace in you, when you will confess the truth.

Faust. But such spirits as can lively resemble   75
Alexander and his paramour shall appear before
your Grace, in that manner that they best lived
in in their most flourishing estate, which I doubt
not shall sufficiently content your imperial Majesty.   80

Emp. Go to, Master Doctor; let me see them
presently.

Kni. Do you hear, Master Doctor, you bring
Alexander and his paramour before the Emperor?

Faust. How then, sir?   85

Kni. I'faith, that's true as Diana turned me to
a stag.

Faust. No, sir, but when Actaeon died he left
the horns for you. Mephistophilis, be gone!

                       Exit Mephistophilis.

Kni. Nay, and you go to conjuring I'll be gone.   90

                          Exit Knight.

Faust. I'll meet with you anon for interrupting
    me so—
Here they are, my gracious Lord.

112-13. there's no haste but good: a proverbial expression warning against overhastiness.

Enter *Mephistophilis* with [*spirits* simulating]
Alexander and his *Paramour*.

Emp. Master Doctor, I heard this lady while
she lived had a wart or mole in her neck. How   95
shall I know whether it be so or no?

Faust. Your Highness may boldly go and see.
[*Emperor sees the mole; then spirits exeunt.*]

Emp. Sure these are no spirits but the true substantial bodies of those two deceased princes.

Faust. Will't please your Highness now to send 100
for the knight that was so pleasant with me here
of late?

Emp. One of you call him forth.

Enter the *Knight* with a pair of horns on his head.

Emp. How now, sir knight! Why, I had thought
thou hadst been a bachelor, but now I see thou 105
hast a wife that not only gives thee horns but
makes thee wear them. Feel on thy head.

Kni. Thou damned wretch and execrable dog,
Bred in the concave of some monstrous rock,
How darest thou thus abuse a gentleman?   110
Villain, I say, undo what thou hast done!

Faust. O not so fast, sir; there's no haste but
good. Are you remembered how you crossed me

114-15. **I have met with you:** I am even with you now; see l. 91.

121. **injurious:** insulting.

124. **straight:** at once; see [V.] 80.

in my conference with the Emperor? I think I
have met with you for it.   115

Emp. Good Master Doctor, at my entreaty release him; he hath done penance sufficient.

Faust. My gracious Lord, not so much for the
injury he offered me here in your presence, as to
delight you with some mirth hath Faustus worth-   120
ily requited this injurious knight, which being all
I desire, I am content to release him of his horns.
And, sir knight, hereafter speak well of scholars.
Mephistophilis, transform him straight. Now,
good my Lord, having done my duty I humbly   125
take my leave.

Emp. Farewell, Master Doctor; yet ere you go
expect from me a bounteous reward.

[*Exeunt.*]

Faust, Mephistophilis, and the horse-courser.
From Lycosthenus, *Prodigiorum* (1557).

[**XI.**] S.D. after l. 11. **Horse-Courser:** a dealer in horses.

[SCENE XI]

Enter *Faustus* and *Mephistophilis*.

Faust. Now, Mephistophilis, the restless course
That time doth run with calm and silent foot,
Shortening my days and thread of vital life,
Calls for the payment of my latest years.
Therefore, sweet Mephistophilis, let us   5
Make haste to Wittenberg.
    Meph. What, will you go on horseback or on
      foot?
    Faust. Nay, till I am past this fair and pleasant
      green   10
I'll walk on foot.

Enter a *Horse-Courser*.

Horse-C. I have been all this day seeking one
Master Fustian: mass, see where he is!—God save
you, Master Doctor.
    Faust. What, horse-courser, you are well met.   15
    Horse-C. Do you hear, sir, I have brought you
forty dollars for your horse.
    Faust. I cannot sell him so; if thou likest him for
fifty, take him.

23. **charge:** responsibility.

27-8. **ride him not into the water:** being a magic creation, the horse will vanish if taken into running water; **at any hand:** no matter what happens.

37. **quality of hey ding:** high spirits.

41. **water:** urine, for analysis.

Horse-C. Alas, sir, I have no more. [*To Mephi-*   20
stophilis] I pray you speak for me.

Meph. I pray you, let him have him: he is an
honest fellow, and he has a great charge: neither
wife nor child.

Faust. Well, come, give me your money. My   25
boy will deliver him to you; but I must tell you
one thing before you have him: ride him not into
the water at any hand.

Horse-C. Why, sir, will he not drink of all
waters?   30

Faust. O yes, he will drink of all waters, but
ride him not into the water. Ride him over hedge
or ditch, or where thou wilt, but not into the
water.

Horse-C. Well, sir, now am I made man for-   35
ever: I'll not leave my horse for forty. If he had
but the quality of hey ding, hey ding ding, I'd
make a brave living on him: he has a buttock as
slick as an eel. Well, God b'wi'ye, sir, your boy
will deliver him me—but hark ye, sir, if my horse   40
be sick or ill at ease, if I bring his water to you
you'll tell me what it is?

Faust. Away, you villain! What, dost think I
       am a horse-doctor?   *Exit Horse-Courser.*
What art thou, Faustus, but a man condemned   45
       to die?

49. **Confound:** eliminate; **passions:** moods.

50. **call:** save.

51. **conceit:** imagination; see [I.] 82.

53. **Doctor Lopus:** Dr. Roderigo Lopez, physician to Queen Elizabeth, who was convicted of plotting to poison the Queen and was executed for treason in 1594. This is an obvious interpolation inserted after Marlowe's death in 1593.

56. **ruled:** guided.

63. **bottle:** bundle.

66-7. **snipper-snapper:** servant.

67-8. **hey-pass:** sleight-of-hand artist.

Thy fatal time doth draw to final end,
Despair doth drive distrust unto my thoughts.
Confound these passions with a quiet sleep:
Tush, Christ did call the thief upon the cross;   50
Then rest thee, Faustus, quiet in conceit.

Sleep in his chair.

Enter *Horse-Courser* all wet, crying.

Horse-C. Alas, alas, Doctor Fustian quotha—
mass, Doctor Lopus was never such a doctor—
has given me a purgation, has purged me of forty
dollars; I shall never see them more. But yet,   55
like an ass as I was, I would not be ruled by him,
for he bade me I should ride him into no water.
Now I, thinking my horse had had some rare
quality that he would not have had me know of,
I, like a venturous youth, rid him into the deep   60
pond at the town's end. I was no sooner in the
middle of the pond but my horse vanished away,
and I sat upon a bottle of hay, never so near
drowning in my life. But I'll seek out my Doctor
and have my forty dollars again, or I'll make it   65
the dearest horse!—O, yonder is his snipper-snapper. [*To Mephistophilis*] Do you hear, you hey-
pass, where's your master?

75. **glass-windows:** spectacles.

Meph. Why, sir, what would you? You cannot speak with him.   70

Horse-C. But I will speak with him.

Meph. Why, he's fast asleep; come some other time.

Horse-C. I'll speak with him now, or I'll break his glass-windows about his ears.   75

Meph. I tell thee, he has not slept this eight nights.

Horse-C. And he have not slept this eight weeks I'll speak with him.

Meph. See where he is fast asleep.   80

Horse-C. Ay, this is he. God save ye, Master Doctor. Master Doctor! Master Doctor Fustian! Forty dollars, forty dollars for a bottle of hay!

Meph. Why, thou seest he hears thee not.

Horse-C. So ho ho! So ho ho! *Hallow in his ear.* 85
No, will you not wake? I'll make you wake ere I
go.   *Pull him by the leg, and pull it away.*
Alas, I am undone! What shall I do?

Faust. O my leg, my leg! Help, Mephistophilis: call the officers! My leg, my leg!   90

Meph. Come, villain, to the Constable.

Horse-C. O Lord, sir, let me go, and I'll give you forty dollars more.

Meph. Where be they?

96. **ostry:** hostelry, inn.

Horse-C. I have none about me; come to my 95
ostry and I'll give them to you.

Meph. Be gone quickly.

　　　　　　　Horse-Courser runs away.

Faust. What, is he gone? Farewell he! Faustus
has his leg again, and the horse-courser, I take it,
a bottle of hay for his labor. Well, this trick shall 100
cost him forty dollars more.

Enter *Wagner.*

How now, Wagner, what's the news with thee?

Wag. Sir, the Duke of Vanholt doth earnestly
entreat your company.

Faust. The Duke of Vanholt!—an honorable 105
gentleman, to whom I must be no niggard of my
cunning. Come, Mephistophilis, let's away to
him.

　　　　　　　　　　Exeunt.

[XII.] 13. **meat:** food.

[SCENE XII]

Enter *Faustus* and *Mephistophilis* with the *Duke*
and *Duchess of Vanholt.*

Duke. Believe me, Master Doctor, this merriment hath much pleased me.

Faust. My gracious Lord, I am glad it contents
you so well. But it may be, Madam, you take no
delight in this. I have heard that great-bellied   5
women do long for some dainties or other: what
is it, Madam? Tell me, and you shall have it.

Duch. Thanks, good Master Doctor; and for I
see your courteous intent to pleasure me, I will
not hide from you the thing my heart desires,   10
and were it now summer, as it is January and
the dead time of the winter, I would desire no
better meat than a dish of ripe grapes.

Faust. Alas, Madam, that's nothing. Mephistophilis, be gone!   [*Exit Mephistophilis.*]   15
Were it a greater thing than this, so it would
content you you should have it.

18. **on:** of.
25. **circles:** hemispheres.
27. **Saba:** Sheba; see [V.] 203.

[Re-]enter *Mephistophilis* with the grapes.

Here they be, Madam: will't please you taste on
them?

Duch. Believe me, Master Doctor, this makes 20
me wonder above the rest, that being in the dead
time of winter and in the month of January, how
you should come by these grapes.

Faust. If it like your Grace, the year is divided
into two circles over the whole world, that when 25
it is here winter with us, in the contrary circle
it is summer with them, as in India, Saba, and
farther countries in the East, and, by means of a
swift spirit that I have, I had them brought
hither as ye see. How do you like them, Madam? 30
be they good?

Duch. Believe me, Master Doctor, they be the
best grapes that e'er I tasted in my life before.

Faust. I am glad they content you so, Madam.

Duke. Come, Madam, let us in, 35
Where you must well reward this learned man
For the great kindness he hath showed to you.

Duch. And so I will, my Lord, and whilst I live
Rest beholding for this courtesy.

Faust. I humbly thank your Grace. 40

Duch. Come, Master Doctor, follow us and
receive your reward. *Exeunt.*

Man with death and a demon.
From Fabio Glissenti, *Discorsi morali . . . contra il dispiacer del morire* (1600).

[SCENE XIII]

Enter *Wagner* solus.

Wag. I think my master means to die shortly
For he hath given to me all his goods;
And yet methinks if that death were near
He would not banquet, and carouse, and swill
Amongst the students, as even now he doth,   5
Who are at supper with such belly-cheer
As Wagner ne'er beheld in all his life.
See where they come: belike the feast is ended.
                                        [*Exit.*]

Enter *Faustus* and *Mephistophilis* with two or
three *Scholars.*

1. Sch. Master Doctor Faustus, since our conference about fair ladies, which was the beauti-   10
fullest in all the world, we have determined
with ourselves that Helen of Greece was the ad-
mirablest lady that ever lived. Therefore, Master
Doctor, if you will do us that favor as to let us
see that peerless dame of Greece whom all the   15
world admires for majesty, we should think ourselves much beholding unto you.
Faust. Gentlemen,
For that I know your friendship is unfeigned,

Paris and Helen.
From *Promptuarii iconum* (1553).

23. **otherways:** different.
25. **Dardania:** Troy.
31. **rape:** abduction.

And Faustus' custom is not to deny   20
The just requests of those that wish him well,
You shall behold that peerless dame of Greece,
No otherways for pomp and majesty
Than when Sir Paris crossed the seas with her
And brought the spoils to rich Dardania.   25
Be silent, then, for danger is in words.
Music sounds, and Helen passeth over the stage.
   2. *Sch*. Too simple is my wit to tell her praise
Whom all the world admires for majesty.
   3. *Sch*. No marvel though the angry Greeks
      pursued   30
With ten years' war the rape of such a queen
Whose heavenly beauty passeth all compare.
   1. *Sch*. Since we have seen the pride of
      Nature's works
And only paragon of excellence,   35
Let us depart, and for this glorious deed
Happy and blessed be Faustus evermore.
   Faust. Gentlemen, farewell; the same I wish
      to you.

                    [*Exeunt Scholars*.]

            Enter an *Old Man*.

   Old Man. Ah, Doctor Faustus, that I might   40
      prevail
To guide thy steps unto the way of life,

47. **heaviness:** sorrow.
50. **flagitious:** extremely wicked.
58. **right:** its due, according to Faustus' contract.
64. **grace:** divine grace.

By which sweet path thou mayst attain the goal
That shall conduct thee to celestial rest!
Break heart, drop blood, and mingle it with 45
  tears—
Tears falling from repentant heaviness
Of thy most vile and loathsome filthiness,
The stench whereof corrupts the inward soul
With such flagitious crimes of heinous sins 50
As no commiseration may expel
But mercy, Faustus, of thy Saviour sweet,
Whose blood alone must wash away thy guilt.
  Faust. Where are thou, Faustus? Wretch, what
    hast thou done? 55
Damned art thou, Faustus, damned! Despair
  and die.
Hell calls for right, and with a roaring voice
Says, "Faustus, come; thine hour is come!"
And Faustus will come to do thee right. 60
              Mephistophilis gives him a dagger.
  Old Man. Ah stay, good Faustus, stay thy des-
    perate steps!
I see an angel hovers o'er thy head,
And with a vial full of precious grace,
Offers to pour the same into thy soul: 65
Then call for mercy and avoid despair.
  Faust. Ah my sweet friend, I feel thy words
To comfort my distressed soul.

70-1. **with heavy cheer:** i.e., sorrowfully; see l. 47.

79. **Revolt:** i.e., against God.

85. **drift:** lack of resolution.

87. **crooked age:** i.e., the old man.

88. **durst:** dared.

Leave me awhile to ponder on my sins.

   Old Man. I go, sweet Faustus, but with heavy   70
     cheer,

Fearing the ruin of thy hopeless soul.   [*Exit.*]

   Faust. Accursed Faustus, where is mercy now?

I do repent and yet I do despair:

Hell strives with grace for conquest in my breast.   75

What shall I do to shun the snares of death?

   Meph. Thou traitor, Faustus, I arrest thy soul

For disobedience to my sovereign lord.

Revolt, or I'll in piecemeal tear thy flesh.

   Faust. Sweet Mephistophilis, entreat thy lord   80

To pardon my unjust presumption,

And with my blood again I will confirm

My former vow I made to Lucifer.

   Meph. Do it then quickly with unfeigned heart

Lest greater danger do attend thy drift.   85

   Faust. Torment, sweet friend, that base and
     crooked age

That durst dissuade me from thy Lucifer,

With greatest torments that our hell affords.

   Meph. His faith is great: I cannot touch his   90
     soul;

But what I may afflict his body with

I will attempt, which is but little worth.

   Faust. One thing, good servant, let me crave
     of thee

   95

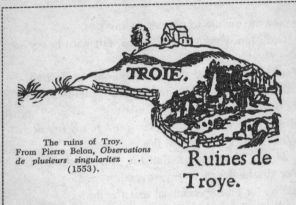

The ruins of Troy.
From Pierre Belon, *Observations de plusieurs singularitez* . . . (1553).

Ruines de Troye.

108. **Ilium:** Troy. The "topless towers" were the high fortified walls of the city.

116. **Menelaus:** king of Lacedaemon, Helen's husband.

Menelaus.
From *Promptuarii iconum* (1553).

To glut the longing of my heart's desire:
That I might have unto my paramour
That heavenly Helen which I saw of late,
Whose sweet embracings may extinguish clean
These thoughts that do dissuade me from my   100
   vow,
And keep mine oath I made to Lucifer.
   Meph. Faustus, this, or what else thou shalt
      desire
Shall be performed in twinkling of an eye.   105

Enter *Helen*.

   Faust. Was this the face that launched a thou-
      sand ships
And burnt the topless towers of Ilium?
Sweet Helen, make me immortal with a kiss.
Her lips sucks forth my soul—see where it flies!   110
Come, Helen, come, give me my soul again.
Here will I dwell, for heaven is in these lips
And all is dross that is not Helena.

Enter *Old Man* [and silently looks on].

I will be Paris, and for love of thee
Instead of Troy shall Wittenberg be sacked,   115
And I will combat with weak Menelaus
And wear thy colors on my plumed crest;

118. **Achilles:** the Greek hero, famed for his prowess, who took part in the siege of Troy. His mother had sought to make him immortal by dipping him in the Styx when he was a child, but the heel by which she held him remained unimmersed and therefore vulnerable.

122. **flaming Jupiter:** chief of the gods and lord of heaven. At the request of Semele, with whom he was in love, he appeared to her in his guise of lord of thunder and lightning, and Semele was consumed.

125. **wanton Arethusa:** a nymph, beloved of the river god Alpheus. Diana preserved her from his pursuit by changing her to a fountain. The adjective "wanton" possibly refers to the playful waters of the fountain and the "monarch of the sky" may be either Phoebus, the sun god, or the moon goddess, sometimes known as Semele, pictured as reflected in Arethusa's waters.

130. **sift:** test.

134. **state:** power.

Yea, I will wound Achilles in the heel
And then return to Helen for a kiss.
O thou art fairer than the evening air   120
Clad in the beauty of a thousand stars!
Brighter art thou than flaming Jupiter
When he appeared to hapless Semele,
More lovely than the monarch of the sky
In wanton Arethusa's azured arms,   125
And none but thou shalt be my paramour!
                    Exeunt all except the Old Man.
  Old Man. Accursed Faustus, miserable man,
That from thy soul excludest the grace of heaven
And fliest the throne of his tribunal seat.

        Enter the *Devils* to torment him.

Satan begins to sift me with his pride.   130
As in this furnace God shall try my faith,
My faith, vile hell, shall triumph over thee!
Ambitious fiends, see how the heavens smiles
At your repulse, and laughs your state to scorn.
Hence, hell! for hence I fly unto my God.   135
                            Exeunt.

Achilles.
From *Promptuarii iconum* (1553).
(See [XIII.] 118.)

[XIV.] 4. **still:** always.
10. **surfeit:** that is, too much food.

[SCENE XIV]

Enter *Faustus* with the *Scholars*.

Faust. Ah, gentlemen!

1. Sch. What ails Faustus?

Faust. Ah, my sweet chamber-fellow, had I
lived with thee then had I lived still, but now I
die eternally. Look! comes he not? comes he not? 5

2. Sch. What means Faustus?

3. Sch. Belike he is grown into some sickness by
being over-solitary.

1. Sch. If it be so, we'll have physicians to cure
him; 'tis but a surfeit, never fear, man. 10

Faust. A surfeit of deadly sin that hath damned
both body and soul.

2. Sch. Yet, Faustus, look up to heaven: remember God's mercies are infinite.

Faust. But Faustus' offense can ne'er be par- 15
doned; the Serpent that tempted Eve may be
saved, but not Faustus. Ah, gentlemen, hear me
with patience, and tremble not at my speeches.
Though my heart pants and quivers to remember
that I have been a student here these thirty years, 20

Jupiter, controller of thunder and lightning.
From Vincenzo Cartari, *Imagini de gli dei delli antichi* (1615).
(See [XIII.] 122.)

74

O would I had never seen Wittenberg, never
read book! And what wonders I have done all
Germany can witness, yea all the world, for
which Faustus hath lost both Germany and the
world, yea heaven itself—heaven the seat of God,   25
the throne of the blessed, the kingdom of joy,
and must remain in hell forever, hell, ah hell,
forever! Sweet friends, what shall become of
Faustus, being in hell forever?

3. Sch. Yet, Faustus, call on God.   30

Faust. On God, whom Faustus hath abjured?
on God, whom Faustus hath blasphemed? Ah,
my God, I would weep, but the Devil draws in
my tears! Gush forth, blood, instead of tears,
yea, life and soul. O he stays my tongue; I would   35
lift up my hands but, see, they hold them, they
hold them!

All. Who, Faustus?

Faust. Lucifer and Mephistophilis.
Ah, gentlemen, I gave them my soul for my cun-   40
ning.

All. God forbid!

Faust. God forbade it indeed, but Faustus
hath done it: for vain pleasure of twenty-four
years hath Faustus lost eternal joy and felicity.   45
I writ them a bill with mine own blood, the date

Satan.
From *The Book of Magic* (c. 1580). Folger MS. V.b.26.

is expired, the time will come, and he will fetch me.

1. Sch. Why did not Faustus tell us of this before, that divines might have prayed for thee? 50

Faust. Oft have I thought to have done so, but the Devil threatened to tear me in pieces if I named God, to fetch both body and soul if I once gave ear to divinity; and now 'tis too late. Gentlemen, away, lest you perish with me. 55

2. Sch. O what shall we do to save Faustus?

Faust. Talk not of me, but save yourselves and depart.

3. Sch. God will strengthen me: I will stay with Faustus. 60

1. Sch. Tempt not God, sweet friend, but let us into the next room, and there pray for him.

Faust. Ay, pray for me, pray for me! And what noise soever ye hear, come not unto me, for nothing can rescue me. 65

2. Sch. Pray thou, and we will pray that God may have mercy upon thee.

Faust. Gentlemen, farewell. If I live till morning I'll visit you; if not, Faustus is gone to hell.

All. Faustus, farewell. *Exeunt Scholars.* 70
                    The clock strikes eleven.

Faust. Ah, Faustus,
Now hast thou but one bare hour to live

Ovid.

From Jean de Tournes, *Insignium aliquot virorum icones* (1559).

76. **Nature's eye:** the sun.

80. **lente lente currite noctis equi:** "run slowly, slowly, horses of the night," a quotation from Ovid, *Amores,* I.13.

And then thou must be damned perpetually!
Stand still, you ever-moving spheres of heaven,
That time may cease and midnight never come;   75
Fair Nature's eye, rise, rise again, and make
Perpetual day; or let this hour be but
A year, a month, a week, a natural day,
That Faustus may repent and save his soul!
O lente lente currite noctis equi.   80
The stars move still, time runs, the clock will
    strike,
The Devil will come, and Faustus must be
    damned.
O I'll leap up to my God! Who pulls me down?   85
See, see, where Christ's blood streams in the fir-
    mament!—
One drop would save my soul—half a drop! ah,
    my Christ!
Ah, rend not my heart for naming of my Christ;   90
Yet will I call on him—Oh, spare me, Lucifer!
Where is it now? 'Tis gone; and see where God
Stretcheth out his arm and bends his ireful brows.
Mountains and hills, come, come and fall on me
And hide me from the heavy wrath of God.   95
No, no—
Then will I headlong run into the earth:
Earth, gape! O no, it will not harbor me.
You stars that reigned at my nativity,

Pythagoras.
From Jean de Tournes, *Insignium aliquot virorum icones* (1559).

114. **wanting:** lacking.

116. **Pythagoras' metempsychosis:** the theory formulated by Pythagoras of the transmigration of souls from one living creature to another at death.

Whose influence hath allotted death and hell, 100
Now draw up Faustus like a foggy mist
Into the entrails of yon laboring cloud
So that my soul may but ascend to heaven.

The watch strikes.

Ah, half the hour is past;
'Twill all be past anon. 105
O God,
If thou wilt not have mercy on my soul,
Yet for Christ's sake whose blood hath ransomed
me
Impose some end to my incessant pain: 110
Let Faustus live in hell a thousand years,
A hundred thousand, and at last be saved!
O, no end is limited to damned souls.
Why wert thou not a creature wanting soul?
Or why is this immortal that thou hast? 115
Ah, Pythagoras' *metempsychosis*—were that true,
This soul should fly from me, and I be changed
Unto some brutish beast.
All beasts are happy, for when they die
Their souls are soon dissolved in elements, 120
But mine must live still to be plagued in hell.
Cursed be the parents that engendered me!
No, Faustus, curse thyself, curse Lucifer
That hath deprived thee of the joys of heaven.

The clock strikes twelve.

134. **full:** completely.

135. **Apollo's laurel bough:** symbol of learning, since Apollo was the god of learning.

136. **sometime:** at one time, formerly.

142. **Terminat hora diem, terminat author opus:** as the hour ends the day, the author ends his work.